Sea Queen Reborn

A Little Mermaid Retelling

RHEA RYAN

Blurb

Sea Queen: Reborn
A Dark Fairy Tale Retelling

To discover the truth of my sister's demise, I must infiltrate the legendary Pearl Castle. The home of ancient magic and ruthless Atlantean Kings. Fueled by a thirst for revenge, my path is paved with bloodshed. As I get swept away by the castle's irresistible charms, treachery threatens to expose my true identity and I undergo a transformation that will shape my destiny. Now faced with imminent danger, will love and power be enough to save me from destruction?

Trigger Warnings
Non-Con

Choking
Torture
Captivity
Violence
Death

Chapter One

OPHELIA

Three days, no more, no less. That is how long Papa let me stay anywhere. Today marks my fourth day in Atlantis. I came here after my father's death. It's the closest place to home, as it's where I last saw my sister alive.

Now I am afraid, angry, and utterly alone.

We are traveling sea merchants, and Papa died from catching a mysterious illness while onboard a ship. So now, it's just me and the small wagon that harbors my few precious possessions. I left it at a camp with our horse and paid some men there to tend it and keep it for me while I'm away.

My determination is steady as I make my way up the steep, jagged rocky steps that lead up the mountain to the entrance of the castle. Its towering spires and gilded wall overlook the marvelous city below. The fiery sun sets on the horizon, blending into the vast ocean beyond. My heart is broken from losing my father, but it's anger that fuels me forward. My desire for revenge.

Are you sure about this, Ophelia?

Papa's words echo in my mind.

He'd disapprove of my actions if he knew what I'm about to do. After all, he went to great lengths to protect me—to hide me. The castle is unfriendly, especially to an oceanid.

I march forward anyway.

Step by step, I try to control my beating heart. It's not plainly evident I am from the ocean realm, as I've spent most of my life on land. Although, when the ocean calls me, every fiber of my being responds. When I'm near water, my skin tingles. My true nature dying to come out. But on land, I look just like them—*human.* Which makes me entirely unique. The number of us is uncertain. If the royals learn of a man having sex with a siren, it's punishable by death.

That's exactly what my father did—twice.

Luckily, he never got caught and kept us hidden. Well, at least me anyway, but my sister wasn't so lucky.

I approach the massive drawbridge. Its iron gates loom in front of me. My heart sinks. It's closed as if to remind me I don't belong here. Steep rock cliffs cover each side, barring any other way in. No matter what happens, I must stay strong in my resolve and find out what happened to my sister, Brielle.

To my relief, the draw bridge lifts as I step near it. The chains grind together as the planks lower and gates open.

Yes, Papa. I'm sure about this.

I'm not surprised by the added measures of protection. The royals have a reputation for hostility and violent behavior, especially to those they deem enemies. Tensions are rising in the south and a war is brewing. I feel it in the air, in my bones, and in the magic of the Coral Throne, cackling around me.

Tension—power—war.

Whispers scatter among the city folk, and the sailors are especially rowdy. Their knives are as sharp as their tongues. They drank every drop of ale the past couple of nights, many beating each other to a bloody pulp to unleash their pent-up anger and displeasure.

A stone staircase crested on the mountain greets me as I step inside the gate. Coral structures are etched into the rocky stone, a mark of beauty from generations past when Atlantis was at peace and the rulers gave grace upon its subjects. Unlike the pathetic excuse of the king, who now rules us. I step up the stairs and approach the towering castle above. A mighty fortress always prepared for battle, and I'm walking right in as an enemy hidden among them.

As dusk approaches, the city behind me glows. I'm supposed to meet him at sunset—the mystery man from last night I met at the tavern in the city below. He's waiting for me now, I'm sure. Tall, dark, and so handsome with soft lips I will never forget. He didn't belong in that dingy place, usually reserved for crooks, thieves, and scoundrels. Despite his best efforts to blend in, he was too pretty and sophisticated. I knew right away he was different.

As I walk up the steps, the castle hums around me. The vibrations cause the hair on my arms to prickle and my belly to stir. I've not been here before, but it's an essence I recognize deep within my soul, an ancient whisper that pulses through me.

It's a part of me.

The Throdos family wields the power of the Coral Throne. It's a keeper of the magic bestowed upon them by the Creator himself and is said to protect them. It runs through the walls of the castle;

it lives and breathes as if it too is a sentient creature. The magic is the soul of the Creator, the same mighty power that purrs in my blood.

The ocean breeze picks up. So, I gather my long, silky, black hair, pull it back to keep it from gusting in the wind, and I keep going.

Up, up, up.

Like I'm walking into the heavens, even though I'm certain this place is the portal to hell. The castle doors open, and a dark figure emerges from the glowing light within. It's him, Sebastian, the man from last night, greeting me as he said he would.

He flashes me with a smile and an arch of a well-manicured brow. "Ophelia, welcome to Pearl Castle." He reaches his hand out, and I slide my fingers into his, letting him guide me in.

Past the threshold.

No one gets into the castle without being invited. I ignore the tingle between my legs as he presses his lips to my hand and slides his fingers to the small of my back.

He's just as handsome as he was last night and a few years my senior. Well dressed with onyx hair that still seems to shine in the light. His dark blue eyes are cunning as he beholds me. His stare lingers on the pearls that hang down the deep cut of my dress. While he is pleasant, he is only a distraction and not the real reason I'm here.

My cheeks flush as I remember all the places his lips and hands touched me last night in our moment of stolen kisses in the dark halls behind the tavern. I sang for the sailors, as I do in every town I visit. Most nights, I enjoy having them satisfy my needs. Their scars make me salivate, and the way their knives hang off their belts reminds me of how rough and strong they are. I take pleasure in the way they gaze at me while I trace my fingers over their sea creature tattoos that adorn their arms, necks, and faces. I can bring these powerful men to their knees when I sing. Especially late at night when I wrap my lips around their cocks and become the center of their world.

Most of the time, they leave me money after they fuck me.

It's enough to survive, and if Papa knew what I was doing, he never brought it up. Especially since I always left some of those coins for him, too.

Last night, though, it was Sebastian who followed me in the dark. He kept to the shadows. I hadn't noticed him earlier, but he was clearly watching me. I'm so glad he did because he couldn't take his hands off me. He mentioned he worked in the castle, and the court needed new entertainment.

After our kisses, he excused himself and left me reeling for more. So, I ended up taking a sailor home to my bed, because I was so lusty from the dark stranger. Tonight, however, instead of spending another night spreading my legs and singing for the seafaring folk, I accepted his offer. He invited me into the castle, my exact goal when I came to Atlantis to begin with.

I give him a sweet smile and a curtsy. "Thank you, your Grace."

Sebastian snickers. "Oh no, dear Ophelia, I may have royal blood, but I am not graceful. Save your pleasantries for my cousins, I am a mere adviser." He licks his lips and trails his eyes up and down the slit in my dress. "Call me Bash."

My heart twitches. Bash is a royal, just as I suspected when I saw him with his flash of jewels hanging around his neck.

I smile at him through my thick, dark lashes. "Bash then."

I took great care in making sure I looked perfect this evening.

I chose a backless coral gown that has slits that rise to my upper thighs, leaving little to the imagination. I stole it from a rich woman on my travels. It's one of two I own, and I've never had the opportunity to wear something so lovely in my twenty-one years.

Bash leads us farther inside the castle, and my breath is stolen away. The entrance is a spacious oval room with arched windows to take in the magnificent view. At its center, tall coral columns support the high domed ceiling. The marble floor has an interactive pattern of mosaics that also cover the walls.

The throne itself is a grand, ornate chair made of seashells and pearls. Behind it, an open aired window overlooking the ocean beyond. I resist the urge to sit on it as it purrs at me.

My blood sings in its presence.

Two slender, towering men with hooked noses and jet-black hair make their way toward us. They are dressed in matching dark suits with skin that is almost translucent, like they've never seen the light of day. Identical twins—with an insidious stare.

Bash quirks his lips. "Ophelia, this is Atticus. They are at your service for anything you may require while in the castle."

They bow at the same time.

Bash continues, "Please meet your castle stewards."

I narrow my brow, and Bash cuts me off before I can ask the most obvious of questions. "One name—that's all they need, Ophelia."

They—he—*Atticus* laughs.

A feeling not unlike a worm works its way through my insides. They—*he* jerks his head. Every motion, every blink, every breath in unison. What kind of strange magic is this? I don't like it. It's like they have one brain in addition to their strange features.

Bash smiles as he watches the look of wonder on my face, as if

Atticus is completely normal. "Please take your time to freshen up, Ophelia. We dine in an hour—you will be our evening entertainment."

My eyes shoot up. "Wait . . . I don't have to audition?"

A gleam hints in his eyes. "Dinner will be the audition. If the king and prince like you, you get to stay. If they don't, you leave."

I swallow a pit in my throat.

"You've chosen a good night, Ophelia. King Alexander and Prince Ayden's betrothed are visiting from another kingdom. The Duke of Avalor and his daughters are here for royal business and to spend time with the brothers. We have a very full court." He runs his hands along the length of my arms. "I sincerely hope you get to stay. It's been some time since we've had new blood in the castle."

I suppress a shudder down my spine.

Blood.

These are the same people who drained Brielle. They caught her four years ago within the lands of the castle. The rumors of the royals in Atlantis spread far and wide. They collect the blood of sirens.

With Atticus closely watching me, Bash grabs my hands. "See you soon, Ophelia. I do hope I can get a private show."

Brielle was stupid. She got caught in the nets and traps they have hidden all over these waters. I'm still furious at her for leaving me alone. She was my life, my family, and then she was gone, leaving a gaping hole that used to be my heart. They gutted her and took her inside the castle. I'm unaware of what happened to her after. The fishermen took her away from the water and I never saw her again. They'll regain their royal power by doing the same to me if they ever find out my true identity. Power stolen by the sirens all those thousands of years ago.

The royals are tied to the power of the Coral Throne through magic none of us understand. They somehow lost their ability to control it and it lies dormant within them. The sirens stole a small piece of that power through their seduction and the royals are obsessed with gaining back what was lost to them. That same power runs through my veins, giving me the song of seduction I inherited from my mother. Along with all the abilities to breathe and swim while underwater with a tail so strong, I could crush a grown man with one lethal swipe. Unlike the royals' abilities, I have full control over mine. It's as natural to me as breathing.

Bash leaves me with Atticus, who turns and gestures for me to follow them without so much as uttering a word. Although, I catch them casting a look at one another. Perhaps they don't share a brain, after all.

Be careful, Ophelia.

My chest tightens at his warning. *Yes, Papa, I will be careful.*

My singing for the king and his brother will help secure my place in court. I will kill both brothers, then Bash, before they stick their royal cocks inside me. I plan to avenge my sister at all costs. As powerful as my mother is, my father gave me the greatest power of all—human legs. Which means I can easily hide among them.

Right now, I must prepare to give the best performance of my life. I will plan a private show for Bash just for fun. I'm attracted to him, even if I must destroy him, because why can't my revenge be sweet at all?

Chapter Two

BASH

I jog up the spiral staircase of the castle and barge into my cousin Ayden's room. I don't bother knocking. I'm wound too tight. Ayden, who is a younger prince and a higher noble than me, views me as an older brother, and I treat him as if he were my sibling. Although technically, Ayden's brother is my oldest cousin who sits on the Coral Throne. Ayden's brother is King Alexander and combined, we make up the royal family of Atlantis. The Kingdom.

Alexander is a complete fool. I've always thought I've done a superb job pulling strings from behind, and Alex doesn't even realize it. None of the responsibility—all the fun. The view from our rooms is a constant reminder of my position and power over the city.

Prince Ayden has a maid on all fours on the edge of his circular bed when I walk into his grand room. He stands on the floor in front of his bed with his cock hanging out, hard and ready. His room, not unlike my own, has gilded walls cooled by a sea breeze blowing through the open decorative windows. The vast balcony overlooks the sparkling ocean beyond. The wind blows his wavy, golden locks, which hang just below his ears. His baby face is delighted at the young woman readying herself for him. He's always been a simple boy—easy to please and easier to manipulate.

I chuckle at the sight. My younger cousin, barely nineteen, can't seem to keep his cock in his pants for longer than an hour. It reminds me of how I was at his age—spoiled, selfish, and completely oblivious.

Over the years, my tastes have become more refined. *King Alexander* has tried and miserably failed at keeping me at bay. Ayden is becoming more like me by the day, and I know his royal fucking highness doesn't like it one bit. Alex likes to keep his discretions secret and encourages us to do the same to not soil his reputation among the kingdoms.

The maid's wet peach greets me and momentarily springs my cock to life as I take in who Ayden is fucking today. I ignore the stir that trembles through me.

Ayden turns his head toward me and arches a brow, and a flash of annoyance hits his eyes. "What is it, cousin? Can't you see I'm busy?" His scowl quickly turns into a grin. "Unless you want your turn?"

The maid turns her head to see what's stopping him from entering her and smiles when she sees me. She wiggles her hips and licks her lips in greeting. I'm not wasting my energy with her tonight, and neither should Ayden.

Not when we can have caviar instead of tuna.

The maid is used goods. We've fucked her silly for months. She's boring—and Poseidon only knows what Alex does with her behind closed doors. He never lets us watch or join, and curiosity kills me. While Ayden and I like to fuck them together, Alex likes his women alone. I just see the aftermath of when they leave. It's a frightening sight, and the shrieks from his rooms are blush worthy.

I stride up to the bed just as Ayden penetrates the maid from behind while she moans and arches her back. He's much softer with ladies than I am. He is a true lover—not a mean bone in his body. The darkness in his blood has not yet emerged as it has with me and Alex. Give it some time, I'm sure that will change, as it did with both Alex and me as the power within our blood festers and stirs.

I slide up on the bed as he hits her deep and I grab her hair, pulling her up to look at me. Unlike Ayden, I am not as gentle. Her big, round, brown eyes glisten as she gets piled from behind.

Fuck.

I'm a tad turned on now.

I pull out my hardening cock, yank her head up, and shove it into her mouth. "There you go, you little whore. Is this what you desire?"

A breathy moan releases as she wraps her lips at the base of my cock, pulling her tongue up its length like I taught her. She pulls off and licks her lips. "Yes," she murmurs. "You're exactly what I desire."

I pull her head up to meet my sharp gaze. "Yes, what?"

"Yes, my king," she says as my cock fills the length of her throat.

Ayden rolls his eyes.

I must confess, outside of the bedroom, I may have no power. In the bedroom, I need absolute authority. I'm the one they bow to.

It's only appropriate. I am, after all, the true king, even if our beloved King Alexander doesn't care to be reminded of that. My cock swells as her lips suck hard. More from her submission than anything else.

"Much better. Don't forget your place," I tell her.

These sluts get so fucking complacent. It drives me crazy, but I thoroughly enjoy reminding them of how I like it. Breaking them down is my favorite part, which is why I'm so bored. Every woman that frequents my bed is now under my complete submission. I no longer have a challenge—until tonight.

With my eyes shut, I let the maid suck as Ayden does his thing with her on the other end. But it's Ophelia's bright red lips I want wrapped around me. I want to run my fingers through her long raven hair and pull it until she screams. Suck on Ophelia's tight little tits till they bleed, and chew on her pussy until she's tortured. Then I plan to come on her pearly white face after I bury myself inside her.

No part of me wants this castle maid whore whose loyalty is questionable as she hops from bed to bed between all three of us. I open my eyes, catching Ayden's gaze. "There is a new girl joining our court. She's a singer I found at the tavern last night."

Ayden pauses and flicks his blonde hair out of his eyes. That catches his attention. I know he'd love to frequent the tavern with me, but Alexander won't allow it. I have much more freedom. Alex gave up on me years ago. He doesn't care who I fuck.

"Alex won't let any new ladies in court right now. Not with the Duke in town—we need to behave, Bash," he says.

Behave—like he is as his betrothed rests in her chambers.

Naughty little Ayden.

Alex won't turn away someone as beautiful as Ophelia. I know him. He will want her, eventually. She will be the new crowned jewel, especially when he hears a voice that sounds like it's from the ocean.

My eyes flicker. "This one's different, Ayden. She's special."

Ayden grunts as he grips the maid's waist, and she shifts, giving him better access as he thrusts deeper into her. The maid bites down on me.

"Fuck," I yell out and pull out of her as a shooting pain hits my gut.

She stares up at me with her eyes narrowed, and I yank her hair up. "You jealous little cunt."

"Calm down, Bash." Ayden brings me back from the brink.

Ayden has never understood the source of my anger—the wild rage that seeps through my bones. Why would he? *He* never lost anything. I can't fault *him* for it. He has a point, though; this maid is not worth my energy. I will punish her later.

I've entirely lost my desire now and my dick tampers down. I will save it for after dinner when I can get Ophelia alone. If Ayden refuses her tonight, even though I'm willing to share, then so be it. It's rare I get to stick my cock into any woman first before the formal royals take their fill. I zip up my pants and pat Ayden on the back as I take my leave. He's ramming into the maid so hard he barely knows I've left.

I snicker as moans fill the room behind me. Just wait until he sees Ophelia. The way she let me taste her last night and invited my hands on her, I can only imagine what her wet pussy feels like. If it's as tight as the rest of her body, I'm in for a real treat.

Ayden has to spend time with his rotten fiancé anyway. A sly grin forms on my lips because Alex's betrothed, the future queen of Atlantis, is hideous too. The royal brothers have to play a game of power and politics tonight, and I know they loathe it.

But as a young king, with Alex only recently taking his throne, our power is fragile. Enemies lurk and vultures circle the castle after the death of my uncle.

After I killed him.

A bold move on my part, but he had to go. I saw my chance, and I took it. It's rare the former king was ever alone. Ever since usurping my father from the throne, he's had a certain level of paranoia. Especially with me—the true heir.

Funny how things go full circle. I killed him the exact same way he killed my father—tossing him off the balcony.

While Alex affords me a good life full of riches, women, and all the wine and gives me the formal position as the Royal Adviser, it's not enough. I do my job, obliging him when he snaps his fingers and do my royal duties. Since he became king something has stirred within me. The Coral Throne beckons me as if it knows Alex should not be the Throdos to reside upon it. For the first time since my father died, I have a longing, something I've never wanted until now. To claim my rightful place as the King of Atlantis.

Chapter Three

OPHELIA

The small bedroom Bash gave me is perfect. Subtle furniture compared to the intricacies of the rest of the castle but softer still than the carriage spot I usually sleep in. I'm a simple girl, and this room's view of the sea is enough for me. I'll only sleep in this room if I have to. I have Bash's attention, and I plan on keeping it.

Atticus said he'd return in an hour to get me. I spent that time brushing my hair and listening to the sounds of the ocean as the waves lap up against the jagged rocks in the swirling waters below. The same spot they caught Brielle sits in the distance.

The water beckons me—I won't last long before I will have to transform. My body needs to spend time in both forms. It's a balance I must maintain. If I don't, I get restless, and my joints ache where my gills and fins should be. My heart bleeds for the water.

The sound calms me as I splash water on my face and make sure I look perfect for the royals this evening, while I make plans to burn their kingdom.

Atticus takes me through the dark halls of the castle, which seem to stretch on forever, lit only by lanterns placed on pedestals along the trim. We see no one as we wind our way through. Atticus walks ahead of me, their feet in perfect lockstep. Every few minutes, they look back at me with their creepy, dark stare. The vile look they give me makes my insides curl.

We turn into a dark hall, and a hum of laughter and music echo through the walls. Bash is waiting for me, and I breathe a sigh of relief. His presence brings me a sense of calm that I can't explain and gets me away from being alone with Atticus and their disgusting grin.

Bash loops my arm through his as the twins disappear to some shadowed corner. He looks dashingly handsome—a black suit cut tight, rich jewels hang around his neck. He's got the tall, dark, and brooding look covered perfectly. He may not be in direct line to the throne, but he looks every part royal.

It's too bad he has to die.

I will play with him first; I can't let him go to waste. If Bash looks like this, I'm excited to see the brothers. The prettier they are, the better. It will make my revenge all that more fun. I plan to worm my way into court, gain their trust, and find out what they did to Brielle. Then my voice will seduce them into my trance, and I'll slit their throats one by one, starting with Bash and ending with the king.

Let the wicked royals watch whilst I destroy them.

Bash turns me to face him and glides his hands down my dress, smoothing out any wrinkles. He tilts his head. "You look perfect, Ophelia. You'll fit in wonderfully at court."

His touch is tender—soft and makes my skin tingle under his

fingertips. I smile and hide the tremble in my hands.

"I hope the king likes me," I whisper, but I know he will.

He presses a kiss to my brow, and my body heats from within, remembering how skilled he is with that mouth.

He grabs my chin and says in a calming voice. "It's time to sing, Ophelia."

Everything rides on my ability to perform today. I will use my magic in its place of origin, but I cannot unleash the full power of my voice. They will sense my magic here, so I must release only a sliver of it. Just enough to capture them without them realizing I trapped them in my spell. It's a risk—I don't know how my magic will react here. The skin tightens around my heart; I am risking my life singing here.

Bash loops my arm once more and escorts me inside. Nothing prepares me for the sight I behold. The ballroom has chandeliers like glowing sea creatures. The room is packed with over a hundred of Atlantis's elite and wealthy, eating with silver spoons at circular tables. Chatter, laughter, and music fill the room. Much different from the sailors I usually spend my time with. I don't fit in—nothing about me belongs here.

Bash takes me straight to the king and the king's brother, who are seated at a long table above everyone else, eating their dessert. Two rather dull women sit on either side of them, who barely spare me more than a glance. With a future queen so ugly, I can easily catch the attention of these two most powerful men. Rich clothing and jewels can't hide the hideousness of these sisters. Plain, blemished, skinny faces, and long noses. I notice they've not touched a single morsel of their dessert.

"May I present Lady Ophelia, our evening entertainment," Bash says, and he turns to me. "Lady Ophelia, Prince Ayden Throdos and King Alexander Throdos. The ruler of the Kingdom of Atlantis."

The royals.

I curtsy to each of them, and as I stare at their handsome faces, I wonder which one did the honor of killing Brielle? Given his baby face and soft hands, the prince seems too young. Just like I was when I lost her. It was Bash or the king. I can't yet tell. However, I do plan to find out.

Unlike Bash, the brothers each have golden hair. The king has much sharper features than either of them. He's handsome, but not my usual type. Alexander is older than Bash by a year or two at my estimate, and he wears the crown with ease.

Each royal gives me a subtle nod as they eat at the center of their long table, but I don't miss the gleam in the younger one's eye, nor the look he shares with his cousin. His eyes linger on the pearls resting on my chest before meeting my soft gaze.

I get nothing from the king—his face is that of stone. He hides his emotions behind his well-manicured brows and angular features. Let's see how long that lasts, as I've heard rumors about his vicious temper. His power radiates off him, and it fires at every nerve. My song lights me up from the inside.

Does he feel it too? He must.

Perhaps gaining access to this court won't be as easy as I thought.

My eyes shift to Ayden, who is deep in conversation with his betrothed. His gaze lingering on me no longer. Bash guides me to the side of the room to get ready for entertaining.

He whispers, angling his head toward mine. "That went well."

I look up at him. "They barely looked at me. I was invisible to them."

His hand slides around my waist, and he squeezes. "They noticed you, Ophelia. I can assure you of that. Now they will really notice you."

He leads me to a stage under a moonlight beam that shines through the domed roof above. The royals are all staring at me now, including Bash. I can't look at the brothers should my voice clam up from nerves. My heart is a raging beat in my chest. This is my only opportunity to uncover the truth about my sister and avenge her. So, my eyes find Bash, who gives me an encouraging nod.

And I begin.

My voice cascades across the silent room. I rein in the power, dying to seep out of me. My whole body clenches, trying to control it. Luckily, I spent my whole life practicing the preciseness of my voice. A skill I learned from my mother. She comes to see me sometimes when I'm in my oceanid form. Although, she will never come too close. None of the pure-blooded sirens ever do. They know we are in the human realm, and I don't properly belong in it either.

I lull everyone in my trance. Their eyes close as they sway softly. I'm enchanting the room, and they have no idea what I am doing to them. I keep my gaze on Bash the whole time, and I know I have him when he gives me the same smoldering look he gave me last night. Ravenous—he can't rip his eyes away from me. I receive the same look from everyone when I sing.

Everyone except King Alexander. His eyes remain fixed on me—alert.

He's immune.

Interesting.

I sing my final song and the room returns to normal, continuing on as before with chatting, laughing, and roaring among the rich nobles. Bash comes to me, grasping my arm with his.

"You were marvelous, Ophelia. King Alex gave me the nod. You've secured your place at court. Welcome to Pearl Castle. I know you will enjoy your time here. Each night you will sing. During the day, you must tend to King Alex's betrothed. Lady Alana and her sister, Lady Deirdre."

My eyes dart to the royal table but they don't spare me a glance. *Enjoy indeed.*

Bash whisks me away. "This evening, Ophelia, you will spend some time with me."

An invitation or a demand?

His hand rests on my hips and he turns me to face him. "Come. I wish to dance with you." He escorts me to the center of the room and leads me through a soft embrace. He twirls and whirls me, holds me, and spins me in his arms. People are buzzing around us, but my eyes are fixed on Bash. My body aches for his gentle touch. He leans down and whispers, "The brothers will have their turn with you, Ophelia. You can count on that. But luckily for me right now, I get you all to myself."

Did they do that to my sister? Pass her around and abuse her? The royals despise my kind; I doubt they would have fucked her knowing what she was.

As I dance with Bash, Ayden casts his gaze in my direction. Like a puppy, eying a bone. But he is stuck dancing with his bride-to-be.

Good. Let him look. It will not be hard to get at him.

As Bash continues to twirl me, I lose him. I get lost in the crowd of people dancing merrily around me. Suddenly, I'm face to face with the king.

Alexander tilts his head; the crown sitting heavy upon it. For a moment, his gaze penetrates me—recognition flashes in his eyes. In those eyes, I see a window into his soul, and my body trembles. I feel Brielle's essence within those hateful eyes. I hear her shrieks and feel her torment from when he killed her. I open my mouth to let out a primal scream as I stand paralyzed under his powerful gaze. But I remember where I am, my wits coming back to me. I cannot unleash my power here, at least not yet.

The king murdered my sister. I can feel it in my bones.

My knees weaken and I gasp for a breath as her pain withers within me and crushes my lungs. She cries out from the dead through our sisterly bond. Then, as quickly as she came to me, she's gone and I'm in Bash's arms once more gasping for air. I'm no longer within the king's control. The king is dancing with his future queen, and I wonder for a moment if I imagined the whole thing. I melt into Bash's arms as his eyes etch with concern. I quickly compose myself, as if it didn't happen at all.

As the night goes on, it's just me and Bash, as if we're alone in the room. For me, right now we are. I feel safe with Bash like he will protect me while in this castle.

I can breathe.

The king makes my stomach quiver, so I avoid looking at him. Brielle was always stronger than me, and she didn't survive them. Why do I think I can?

Ayden glances at me often, and I don't return the looks. I focus solely on the handsome man in front of me. As the room thins out, Bash whispers, "Come, let me show you something, Ophelia."

He grabs two goblets of wine and leads me to a room with a balcony overlooking the sea. An emerald pool at the balcony's edge merges with the ocean beyond. Palace lights blend with the celestial night sky and sparkle off the pool. We are alone and my nerves spiral as I cannot go in that water.

He turns to look at me, handing me my drink. He watches as my eyes grow in wonder and desire, masking the terror I really feel.

"Do you like it?" he asks me, slicing his gaze to the magnificent view.

I nod as I look at the water. My senses heightened. My skin purring. "Yes, very much."

He grabs my hand and pulls me closer. "Can you promise me something, Ophelia?"

My head tilts as I take in his ocean eyes and how they contrast with the rest of his darkened features. His eyes resemble the pool that lies before us.

I blink and take a sip of my drink. "What is it?"

"Comply with the royals' demands, especially Alexander. He has somewhat of a reputation and particular desires with his mistresses."

I blink my eyes in confusion. "What do you mean? I'm not a mistress to King Alex. He's barely looked at me, and are they both not engaged?"

A gleam in his eyes. "Oh, but he will. That is why you're here, Ophelia. You must know that?"

I declare innocence. Of course, that's my desire.

He runs his hand down my arm. "Ayden is a lover. Although reckless, he will not hurt you."

I narrow my eyes; a pulse quickens in my heart. "And King

Alexander?"

A deliberate pause. "They call him the wicked heir."

Shivers run down my spine. Evil is what I sensed when I looked upon his eyes and saw into his soul.

"Why is that?" I ask, frowning.

"Because he likes to make women scream." A darkness shines in his eyes as he tells me this. "He will come for you, Ophelia. Sooner rather than later."

My eyes grow wide, not out of fear, but fascination. How does he make women scream? *I look forward to it. Next time I will be ready for him.*

Bash places his wineglass down on a side table near the pool and lounging chairs and grabs my hand. My hand slides up his rock-hard stomach and I place my drink down next to his.

"And you?" I ask, giving him my full attention. "What are you like, Bash?"

With a gentle tug, he draws me in. "Would you like to find out?"

I smile and let out a giggle as I lean my head back, and he runs his tongue along my neck and into my mouth with grace and experience. His hands are strong, and he grips my waist, pulling me closer. Heat pools within my belly as my body presses into his.

I let him kiss me. His hands roam along my sides and up the swells of my breasts. He then slides his hands up to the top of my head, gathering my hair between his fingers. He's gentle and cautious—then he tugs. He pulls my head back with force, lifting my face to meet his. "You wanted to find out, sweet girl. So here I am."

Something flickers inside me, like the wick of a candle. Not once in all my nights entertaining sailors have they manhandled me like this. Oh, they tried, but their bellies were full of ale and their cocks were too limp to be of much use. If they got too bad, I'd sing and bring them back down and slip away.

I hesitate. My eyes widen. He must know my secret—and he would kill me if he knew. Then I remember he can't know, it's not possible. Bash must be like this with women.

Dominant and in control.

I am consumed by the need to find out more. I'm willing to do anything if it means finding out what happened to Brielle. Soon, Bash will know who the real master is. For now, I'll play along because I am officially intrigued.

Chapter Four

BASH

The exact moment when Ophelia's eyes flash in fear are moments I live for. It sends a thrill right through me. It's the instant I know I've won these women over. Notably, if they don't flee in terror.

Ophelia is special—she stayed despite her fear. A smile even hinted at her lips the moment I gripped her. I salivate when I break them down the first time, but it's even more thrilling building them up again. They are usually stronger for it, and I plan to make Ophelia the strongest of them all. She's the most stunning woman I've ever laid eyes on so I'll take extra care to have fun with her. I'll teach this whore what I like and what she can expect from me.

Complete and utter submission and obedience.

Loyalty.

The last one is hard to find. Especially when Alex gets to them first. They're different after Alex, annoyingly so. A darkness resides in him, like it does within all who bear the Throdos name.

It's why all who are crowned king end up as drunks. The power of the Coral Throne is strongest in the one who wears the crown—it consumes them. It's why I didn't want the job when my father died. I've watched Alex darken in the year he's worn it, as it did his father, and my father before him. Each day, he slips further into its grasp. A thousand years of rule has negatively affected our bloodline. It's ruined every king who sits upon it. The magic—while dormant within us is growing more powerful. It can't be unleashed, so it seems to destroy us instead.

Darkness has always been within me.

Ophelia's delightful green eyes glisten as she stares up at me, waiting for what I will do next. My hand is an iron grip on her hair while my other hand grabs her chin and I squeeze her lips together. I do not force women to take part in my dark ways, and so I ask her again. "Are you still sure you want to know what I'm like, Ophelia?"

Her final chance.

Her throat bobs and her delightful perky tits rise and fall with her short breaths. She opens her mouth to speak, but I need to avoid getting lost in her beautiful voice in order to complete my work.

I shove my fingers in her mouth. "My first rule, Ophelia, is you will not speak unless I tell you."

Her knees weaken and my cock pulses. I pull my fingers out and gently wipe them over her lips. "My second rule is when you speak, you must only refer to me as *my king*."

Her eyes sparkle with confusion.

"Do you understand, Ophelia?" She nods.

"Speak."

"Yes, my king."

My cock nearly explodes at hearing her say those words, but her eyes have shifted. Only a flash, but I saw it. A viciousness that wasn't there before. Something about my preferred nickname triggered her. I might have underestimated her resistance. I hear her words, but I need to *believe* her.

As I circle her, my footsteps echo through the room. I breathe in the scent of her perfume while a tingle of anticipation runs down my spine. She has mysterious beauty and grace unlike any that lives in this castle. But malice flickers behind her eyes and her fists clench at her sides.

Something is there within her. *Anger, rage,* and *hatred* that mirrors my own.

I must break her harder than the others. I pause and trace my tongue along my bottom lip, considering my next words. "Do you like to suck cock, Ophelia?"

Her lips quiver.

"Speak."

Her voice is low and broken. "No, my king."

My inner rage consumes me—I see nothing but red when I hear that word.

A door clicks behind me. Atticus has arrived—*good.* These whores do not love Atticus, and why should they? They are creepy and as ancient as the castle itself. At least that's what I think. Atticus served as a castle steward during my father's childhood, as well as mine.

Atticus has always just—*been.*

But he's loyal to me above all others, so I must reward him. They walk toward the balcony and stand in the corner. Ophelia's eyes widen at the sight of them. They like to watch the first time I break someone, and if I'm being honest, I love an audience. Sometimes when I'm feeling generous and the whores are disobedient, I give Atticus a turn. It's always an entertaining show.

Not tonight—not until Ayden gets his fill of her. Especially not with someone so unique, so special.

My eyes cut to them then back to her as I reach my hand and tuck her hair behind her ear. "Take off your clothes, Ophelia, slowly."

She smirks and pulls off her delicious sea-colored dress one strap at a time and lets it fall to the floor around her feet. With her eyes hooded, she then peers up at me with an arched brow. Her eyes glow in the moonlight. "Yes, my king."

Naughty Ophelia isn't wearing any undergarments, and her body is that of a goddess. A perfect, thin frame. Her hair is shiny and black with tiny waves that fall along her supple breasts. However, her beauty doesn't match my rage.

I grab her hair again and yank her down. "Get on your knees, slut." She must learn early on that the word *no* does not please me. She obeys and drops to her knees while I stand over her, peering down. "Lower your head and bow to me."

She presses her forehead on the marble floor. I leave her there and walk toward the couch we have set up for entertaining guests.

I sit and face her. "Now crawl to me, Ophelia, nice and slow."

She turns her head up and moves to her hands and knees, keeping her eyes on me the whole time. The swells of her breasts pulsing up and down as she makes her way toward me.

Heat builds within me as she slithers her naked body along the floor. When she reaches me, I lean forward and pull her chin up. My cock now pulsing beyond comprehension, but my hands are soft and tender. She will learn my hands are capable of both extremes—intense pain and pleasure. I glide my fingers over her face, caressing her perfect ivory skin, and I pull her up to her knees. "Do you want to try again, my sweet?"

She nods, but her gaze drifts to Atticus, whose lips have curled to a smile. I grab her chin and pull her gaze back to me. "Don't worry about them. They will only observe if you listen to me. If not, I may let them have you and be done with you altogether. Would you want that? Do you want me to throw you away, Ophelia?"

A bite of her lip and a gleam in her eye tells me she does not wish for that outcome. She wants me just as much as I want her. My cock is now a painful bulge in my pants and so I pull it out. It throbs as I stare at those ruby, full lips.

Her eyes shoot me a look of daggers. I have not successfully broken her yet, but I can't wait any longer. I need tending to—I've waited long enough, and I still have a fun punishment planned for her. Let her give me that venomous stare while my cock's in her throat.

I grab her head and run my hand down to her chin. "Open your mouth now, my sweet. I want you to lick my shaft from root to tip, then take the whole thing down your throat."

Let's test her gag reflex.

She should be honored to experience me like this. I am no doubt the highest-born man she's ever been with. She opens her mouth wide, and my groin tightens as she sticks out her delectable little tongue. She works her mouth, licking at the root of my shaft, gliding that little tongue all the way up. She takes her sweet time, savoring every lick before taking me inside her. I groan from how tight her lips feel wrapped around me as she stares right into my eyes. Just as I knew she would.

"Fuck, Ophelia," I murmur, shoving myself further inside her. "Your mouth certainly has many talents, doesn't it?"

I thrust my hips, making her whimper as the length of me hits the back of her throat. I grab her head and thrust so hard her eyes water. It's unfortunate Ayden is not here to see this. He'd be all over her.

Perhaps it's good he is not—

He tends to stifle me when I get particular with them. He always says I taint them and he's not wrong. Ayden likes them sweet and pure; his royal blood is not yet stained with poison.

I continue fucking her mouth as she grabs my legs as to not topple over. I am holding her head so tight; I'm not worried about her moving. She takes every inch of me. Even as I forcefully thrash her, she somehow still tickles me with her tongue right at the tip of my cock in the most delightful way. The pressure builds within me, and I pull her mouth off me before I release.

I'm not finished with her yet; I still need to bury myself inside her before the night is done. Our journey together has only just begun.

I rub my fingers along her lips and take in her sweet smell. A blend of her saliva and wetness that's built between her legs.

What a needy little whore.

"Ophelia, my sweet," I say, as I caress her face. "That was near perfection. But you enjoyed that too much, didn't you?"

Her eyebrows rise in feigned innocence.

"You didn't really get punished, did you?" My eyes shift to the pool. "Do you like to swim, Ophelia?"

A flash of emotion twinkles in her pretty green eyes, so quick I almost miss it.

Fear perhaps?

Her reaction entices me. Perhaps I have found the thing to break her. I also wish to see her naked body dripping wet. The pool's vicious potential makes this room enjoyable for me, a perfect playroom by the sea. I run my tongue over my bottom lip and smile as I grab her shoulders.

Her eyes widen. "No, Bash please," She begs.

My rage boils like lava and my voice is darker than the starry night. "I can't stress enough how important it is that you never say that word, Ophelia."

Even Atticus flinches.

She'll regret her decision to say *no* to me. I yank her up and drag her to the pool by her hair. Desperation pours out of her as she thrashes her frail limbs.

It's time to begin her descent.

Ignoring her pleas, and now even more angry with her for her insolence in calling me Bash, I shove her head in the water. She wiggles and struggles beneath my iron grip as I lower my knees to make sure she understands how little effect begging has on me.

She's powerless while in this castle.

I was once the crowned prince—meant to be king. She should always be on her knees for me.

As I keep her head below water, I slide three fingers between her legs and her pussy muscles clamp down on my fingers. She's tighter than I could have imagined.

I ride my fingers harder inside her until her body goes limp and her pussy throbs against my hand, leaking those lovely juices down her leg. After a few seconds, I pull her head up. I don't want to kill her—that's what Alex would do. I am merciful, and I have much more self-control than that. I am superior to him in many ways.

She is mine now. I will keep her and not share her. She is, after all, just a nomad slut I picked up from the tavern.

A complete nobody.

I'll tell the brothers I threw her in the gutter. She'll be mine to torture and pleasure till I'm done with her.

Her eyes are still closed as I pull her head up and lay her on my lap. I jerk my head to Atticus and signal for him to take his leave. He's seen enough. Now it's time to rebuild her. That's something I do alone.

I caress her soft lips and smooth out her dark, wet hair while her angel-like face rests. Her eyes are closed. She must have passed out, but the shallow breaths in her lungs tell me she didn't drown. She must be very skilled at holding her breath.

It's just me and her now as her body moves and she slips back into consciousness. She opens her eyes and gazes up at me. Her emerald eyes twinkle.

She is no longer full of malice or contempt. Now full of fear—just how I like it.

My fingers caress her catlike cheekbone, and I press my lips to her brow. "Would you like to kiss me now, Ophelia?"

Her voice is weak and delicate—unsure. "Yes, my king."

Much better.

I slide my tongue into her mouth. She returns my kiss by nibbling on my mouth. Greedy little girl wants more of me even though I just defiled her. She took her punishment well, though. I pull my lips from hers. "Do you want to come up to my room?"

She turns away from me and shifts her naked body beneath me.

"Well, do you?" I ask again and rub my hands down her silky smooth skin, teasing her nipples with my thumb and finger. I could take her right now if I wished. Her body is pulsing with desire.

Her back arches and her skin ripples. "Yes, please."

A smile forms on my lips as I slide my hands to the folds of her pretty little pussy and graze my finger over the blooms of her breasts.

"You want more pleasure, Ophelia? Did you enjoy what I just did to you?"

She melts in my arms and nods. It's time to show her how much pleasure these hands can give her. That is the difference between me and my cousin, the false king. I take great pride in pleasuring them when they behave. While King Alexander simply revels in their pain.

Chapter Five

OPHELIA

O verwhelming guilt tightens around every bone in my body for wanting Bash as badly as I do, knowing his involvement with Brielle. While I am also consumed by lust and desire for this man.

Bash is everything I want—powerful, dark, handsome, and striking. I'm inexplicably drawn to him, although I might be in too deep with him.

He surprised me. My whole life, no one has ever tried to hurt me or touch me like that. And I want more—I crave more from him.

Most men I fuck are barely coherent when they stick their limp cocks inside me.

No one compares to Bash. A real man, with power and skills beyond my comprehension, and I haven't even had sex with him yet.

I shouldn't accept him hurting me—his family has caused me enough pain. But I do—every part of my body desires his affection, his praise. The joke is on him, trying to drown an oceanid. I had to slump my body just to stop myself from getting bored. But the payoff was worth it when he slid his fingers inside me and then sent the twins away. His eyes softened, and my power trembled at his mere touch.

I don't know how the power of the Coral Throne affects the royals—the Throdos lineage. It is said their family once used the power at will. They were a manifestation of the gods themselves. The legends say the Coral Throne gifted it to them—ordained them. Until my ancestors stole a piece from them. Perhaps that is why I yearn for him so badly? Nothing else makes any sense.

Bash helps me slip my dress back on and gathers me up in his arms. My face and body are still throbbing from him manhandling me, and my pussy is simply tortured waiting for him to do what he promised. I deserve the treatment of a goddess for what he did and the submission I gave him. For the humiliation I endured in front of those vile twins.

He carries me effortlessly through a back door into candlelit halls. The castle is dark and quiet, only the slight hum from the power within its essence. I close my eyes for a few short moments, enjoying the feeling of being carried by him. His beating heart gives me a twisted sense of comfort. I'm tired—exhausted, especially because it's the middle of the night.

Eventually, we stop and he pushes against a panel on the wall, and it creaks open. We step into the glorious candlelit room beyond. I can only assume we are in Bash's private rooms, and they are very much fit for a royal. He has a stunning view of the city and ocean from a large open-air balcony. As soon as the taste of the sea hits my nose, my siren stirs within me.

The stir only makes me more ravenous.

He lies me on his circular bed made of seashells, covered with dark silk sheets that resemble the depths of the ocean, and I've never experienced such comfort. A girl like me never sleeps in this type of luxury. Bash stands over me—his dark blue eyes flare as I peer up at him behind my long lashes.

I beg with my eyes as I arch my back and spread my legs slightly, giving him a peek at what he's ignored thus far. Of course, I could simply sing, own his soul, fuck him, then slit his throat while under my trance—but what fun is that?

"Now Ophelia," he says, as he grasps the straps of my dress and slips it down, exposing my breasts. My nipples are hard for him—ready to be sucked and fondled. He takes his time sliding my dress right down my stomach, my hips, then my legs, carefully rubbing each thigh until he reaches my public bone, and finally my calves and toes. "Do you want me to fuck you now?" he asks.

I arch my back. "Yes."

I want nothing more than to feel the length of his cock deep inside me.

He snickers. "Of course you do. But do you think you've earned it?"

I wet my lips, eager to please, and nod excitedly.

He rubs his knuckles along my face. "I believe you deserve it, Ophelia, my sweet. You sang like a siren tonight."

My chest tightens. *If he only knew.*

He pulls off his clothes and lies on top of me. His cock teasing me, the warmth of his body pressing into me. He wraps his hand around my neck and reaches his head up to my ear. "You will submit to me tonight, Ophelia. You will give me everything I ask for. Is that clear?"

A breathy moan escapes me. "Yes."

He grips my neck tighter. "Yes, what?"

"Yes, my king," I choke out.

He lifts my knees so they are wide, and I prop myself up on my arms. His eyes flicker. "I will take care of you," he murmurs. "While under my control, I promise I will always treat you like a queen. I will bring you to places of pleasure you never thought possible. You will be safe with me."

Safe.

Brielle wasn't safe.

I lift my legs and wrap them around him, conforming my body to his as my insides throb. I'll be safe with him—only if I can hide what I am. There is something about this man, my feelings buried deep within. Feelings I can't seem to control when I'm around him. I want him—I want to submit to him more than I ever dreamed.

"I'll start off gentle," he says.

He kisses me. Long, deep, sensual and skilled. My body tremors at his touch. He leans up and places his hand on the headboard, sliding his fingers deep inside me. My wetness is dripping from him, and he slides his fingers in, teasing me. He moves his kisses to my nipples, giving each the attention they deserve before sliding his tongue down my womanly curves.

His hands slide to my neck, and he squeezes. I jolt and my world darkens. I can't breathe, speak, or think. Panic consumes me as my eyes go fuzzy. Unlike the water where his desired impact fell short, now I have no control.

For a moment, I grab his hands in panic. I can't sing even if I wanted to. My only defenses taken away from me by mere human hands. I'm at the complete mercy of Bash.

He kisses my cheek. "Remember what I told you, Ophelia. Just relax." Bash's words bring me back from the brink.

Without warning and with his hands still wrapped around my throat, he shoves the length of his cock deep inside me. I moan at the pleasure despite my growing panic for air. He loosens his grip only for a moment while he fucks me hard. I take a breath before he pushes me to the brink of death with another squeeze.

"Fuck, Ophelia." He grunts. "I won't last long with how tight you are. Keep fluttering your eyes like that."

I manage a moan as he hits me deeper and harder. A burst of pleasure waves through me as my world grows fuzzy, and the orgasm swirls through me like a monstrous ocean storm. I explode as his hands release my neck along with the pent-up tension in my body. The feeling is so much that I moan and wither in his arms.

I'm still panting when I open my eyes from the brink of bliss and hell he brought me to. Bash is staring at me—his dark, sexy eyebrows are raised. "Did you like that?" he asks in a soft, sensual voice.

I merely nod. Words simply cannot describe how that made me feel—how he makes me feel. He grabs my waist, whips me around, and pulls me on top of him. I straddle him now, and he runs his hands down my naked body, admiring all the lines of my curves. As I run my hands up and down his chest, I can't help but admire his toned, lean, and masculine form. "That pleases me," he says, and my heart tingles. "You will fuck me again, Ophelia. You will ride my cock until it hurts, and your pussy is raw."

I lean forward and take his cock inside me. He smiles as I dance on top of him, flipping my dark hair out of the way as I grind and clench, giving him a show as I fondle my own breasts and smile at him. I'd fuck him all night if he makes me orgasm like that again.

We fuck most of the night in a sultry mix of pleasure and pain. He is a skilled lover, and my insides explode multiple times before I completely pass out on him, and I fully surrender.

Then I feel it—a small sliver of something jumps from him to me when he finally grunts, quivers, and comes deep inside me. It slides inside my bones—my blood.

A tingle.

I know that tingle—it's from the Coral Throne.

It's Bash's power, and now it's mine.

Exhausted, I drape myself over him and close my eyes. He draws circles all over my back and shoulders as my eyes grow heavy and my lust consumes me. He finally lets me rest and so I curl up beside him as he holds me in a soft embrace.

"Sleep tight, my Ophelia," he whispers in my ear, just as I drift off in the comfort of his arms. "We are just getting started, you and I."

In the depths of my consciousness, I am aware of the power I absorbed from him. It coils through me like a mist over the ocean.

When I awaken the next morning, Bash is already gone. I was so tired—so comfortable I didn't even hear him leave. The soft glow of the morning sun seeps through the window, casting a warm and welcoming light into the room. A cool ocean breeze tightens my nipples as I pull the down blanket off me and slide out of bed. My pussy is still throbbing from all its pleasure the night before. Bash was not lying when he said he would give me what I wanted. He gave me so much more.

I feel it still, deep inside me. A new power threaded together and coursing through me. It makes my stomach coil and tighten. I wonder what it means.

I gaze over to the small table beside the bed. He left me a single rose, which I bring to my nose and smile. No man has ever given me a flower, let alone a highborn noble. Still, it pales compared to the true gift Bash gave me. Across the room, he also left a delightful platter of fruits, spreads, and delicious-smelling breads. My heart bursts at the sight of it.

Beside it, a note:

Ophelia,

Thank you for last night. Please make yourself comfortable in my room. Have a bath and rest. You will need it for later. Meet me before dinner and I will give you a personal tour before you sing again for court. Then, Ophelia my sweet, you are all mine again this evening. There will be a guest this time. And remember, even when you bow to Alexander, don't forget who your true king is.

I'm always watching.

Love Bash.

After that performance, I am happy to meet Bash again. If acting like a slut and letting him choke me pleases him—then it too shall please me.

The thought of the king makes me shudder. My blood turns to ice remembering his eye and Brielle's pain as it flooded through them. I heard her screams as if she were living right in my head. I smelt her sweat and the copper scent of her blood. Her fear was as real as my own.

I close my eyes and lie my head back on Bash's glorious pillow and sleep until mid-morning. I'm not in any hurry to leave Bash's scent—his safety.

When I awaken, I stroll out to the balcony to Bash's extravagant royal bath. This luxurious pool makes me feel like his queen. I'll bathe in waters with the essence of flowers and oils to smooth my skin. A luxury I've never experienced before.

I'm taking a massive risk bathing like this—anyone could see me transform. But I'm desperate to feel my fins—my tail, my true form, if only for a minute. The water is calling to me, as it usually does when I'm near it. It's been ages since she's come out to play.

So, I slip into the marble tub. The warm water engulfs me, and as I submerge down to my waist and the soft aromas of junipers fill my nostrils, I breathe in a cleansing breath while my body pulses through its transformation. My tail forms and my body lengthens and shimmers under the morning sun. My mouth gapes open and I let out a gasp; the warmth infusing my body is as euphoric as Bash's tongue.

It's been much too long since I've seen it. My tail is perfection—it shimmers green, blue, and etches of pink. I've always adored the beauty of it, the same colors as both my mother and sister.

I lean down and slide my hand down its length. The tail has a sharp edge, where if needed I could slice any predator of the ocean till it bled out. Which makes sirens the queens of the sea. The most powerful of the oceanid species.

But I'm not merely a siren—I am something else entirely. My power exceeds that of both a siren and a human combined. This morning I awoke something anew. If only I knew what it was.

Remember why you're here, Ophelia.

My father's voice rings in my ears.

Brielle—I'm here for Brielle, not my own selfish desires. I let Bash distract me, but in my defense, things have changed. Fucking a royal gives me powers. This is why the law exists to capture and destroy us. Sirens took those powers a millennium ago. An ancient ruler fell for one of them—that king gave the sirens the power of their song. He gave her a part of himself and created us. Which means this power, whatever it is, is mine forever. I would pass it on to my children, should I ever have any. So now—now I must sleep with every royal in this castle and claim what is mine.

Chapter Six

OPHELIA

O nce clean and refreshed, I make my way out of Bash's rooms and into the narrow, dim-lit halls of the castle. I didn't want to put on my gown, so I grabbed one of his tunics that barely covers my legs and seek my way back to my own quarters.

I barely make it a single step when Atticus comes skulking into view. My hair prickles on end as I pull down the long tunic to cover myself as this . . . *creature* stands before me.

One last little punishment from Bash to tide me over as Atticus stares at me with lust-filled eyes that makes my stomach twist, turn, and roil, remembering how they watched Bash and me last night as he broke me. I'm relieved they didn't see Bash put me back together or the moment I fell under Bash's spell. I'm willing to do anything to be with Bash again, to please him, and find out what power now binds us.

I must delay my plan to avenge Brielle to discover what Bash has planned for me. I deserve a little pleasure after a life of running and ruin. I will dive to the depths of hell if it means feeling his hands on me again.

His lips, his tongue, his muscled body.

My eyes graze to the twins. "Take me to my rooms," I snap. As much as I love wearing Bash's clothes, I need to change into my attire.

They bow and only one of them speaks. "We are to take you to Lady Alana's chambers, as per His Majesty's request." The other steps forward. "The ladies of court have requested your appearance." They finish the sentence in unison. "And you've kept them waiting."

Their voices echo across the hall, chilling me to my very core.

Twisted magic indeed.

I narrow my eyes. "Bash told me to meet him. He will be upset with me if I don't follow his command and I need to change."

They exchange glances and proceed to escort me to my room. They stay outside, giving me only a moment to change before knocking again. Annoyance tugs at my gut, but I follow them out. They lead me to a set of stone stairs in the castle tower. The ornate sculpture twists from bottom to top and I can't help but marvel at it. These walls are as old as Atlantis itself but not as old as the ancient power that created it.

The walls of Pearl Castle are adorned with intricate details that truly showcase its beauty. When I look closer, the carvings on the walls seem to dance.

Love and war, battle and heartbreak.

As I trace my fingers over the stone, my eyes narrow at the sight of a knife protruding from a siren's throat, and the siren lets out a silent scream.

Ophelia.

That stone whispers my name, and a sharp zap pushes right through me. In an instant, my body jolts, and I pull my hand away as if the stone was burning.

Pain—a thousand years in one moment.

I catch my breath as Atticus stops a few feet ahead. A smile upon their lips as they watch me. I glare at them and hiss, and they simply turns toward an exit out of the stairwell. I compose myself, and we enter the main entrance and walk right by the Coral Throne. My blood pulses and powers stir—the pain lingers in my fingers and bones.

The throne beckons me.

I ignore my pulsing desire to sit on it.

When we arrive at Lady Alana's rooms, she is with her sister and a few other ladies I recognize from last night's festivities. Most are more desirable than the future queen and her sister. I suppress a twinge of jealousy, thinking Bash must have taken at least one of these ladies to his bed.

From the looks of the daggers I'm getting, I can bet a pretty seashell it's more than just one. But it's Lady Alana's gaze that penetrates me the hardest.

She is a hideous woman with her harsh pointy nose and chin. A wave of her hand gestures me forward. "Ophelia, is it?" she asks, and I notice she leaves out *Lady* even though I am now a member of this court.

Lady Alana's rooms are in a different wing of the castle, I'm assuming, so she can't hear the moans of the other women coming out of the royals' bedrooms.

My moans.

I curtsy and remember my place. "Lady Alana."

She's not a queen yet, but her room is breathtaking. Ocean views, warm lighting, and intricate tapestries of soft greens and blues. She lounges on a plush, coral-colored armchair sipping tea and nibbling on a variety of sweet things laid out on a table before her. Her room is quite bright compared to Bash's who seems to favor a darker, richer palette.

She reaches out her hand and I grab it, pressing my lips to her wrist. "Welcome to my rooms, Ophelia. We've all been dying to meet you." She runs her hand toward my cheek and the small bruises Bash left on my neck.

Blood drains from my face, the bruises I forgot to cover up.

She gives me a vicious smile and laughs. "You didn't think going off with Bash made you special, did you? Everyone knows what Bash is like. I figured when he whisked you away, he was up to no good. He really is the devil."

And what about your wicked heir, hideous queen? I want to ask her. *Your king's eyes are a portal to hell.*

I sweetly smile. "Bash was a perfect gentleman."

She pauses, then bursts into laughter, and the other ladies follow suit. "Oh, but of course. Be cautious of him, Ophelia. I don't want my ladies involved in his antics." Her gaze cuts to a sulking woman on the corner of the couch. "Don't we, Lady Lillian?"

Pretty Lady Lillian, with her golden ringlets, blazes her soft eyes into me and I meet her wretched glare. At least I found who else Bash has fucked in this group. I send her an equally menacing stare. *Bash is mine. I will not stay away from him.*

Lady Alana gestures for me to sit and luckily doesn't press the subject. Her sister, Lady Deirdre hasn't said a word but moves over to make me a spot.

"Come. Sit," Lady Alana says. "We don't bite. But you need to be warned, Ophelia. Bash appears nice, but he craves power and will manipulate you to serve his own agenda. Don't trust him. I've banned my ladies from sleeping with him."

I cock my head. "Is that so?"

Lady Alana smiles and tilts her head. "That is so. Everyone knows Bash would do anything to take the throne back to his bloodline. He would betray the king the moment he got a chance. Rumor has it, he killed his uncle to get it back. But it didn't work. Alexander ascended and Bash now bows to him. It's our needs you will always tend to. Is that clear, Ophelia? Alexander is your king, and I will be your queen."

Take the throne back? Bash was supposed to be king?

A tingle flickers through me at the thought of Bash being king. A real king, not the pretend one he is in bed.

"Ophelia?"

I flick my gaze at her. "Yes, of course, my lady. And what of King Alex and Prince Ayden?" I dare to ask her. "What are they like?"

She snickers and a flash courses through her eyes. "I will not speak ill of any Throdos save for Bash. They are part of our alliance and are good family friends. The brothers are perfect gentlemen, I can assure you. My sister and I are so lucky to have such dashing, kind men as our future husbands."

She says these words, but I don't believe her scripted response and the void look in her eyes. She doesn't love King Alex any more than King Alex loves her.

"Where did you learn to sing like that?" It's Lady Deirdre's voice that speaks next. Another sweet smile. "My mother taught me when I was a girl."

It's not a lie. In the sea as a child, she sang to me once when she came near. I mimicked her, and that's how I learned of the power I possessed. The sound of her voice was enough to make us keep our distance, for one does not simply speak to a siren. They are deadly—cunning creatures. Sentient but feral and each stunning in their own way.

My mother was curious about us, though. I saw it in her eyes. My father never spoke of her. I'll never know how I was conceived. I only know I belong to her because of her long, silky, dark hair. Same as Brielle's—same as mine.

All eyes are on me, and I can tell these women love gossip, so I keep pressing. "Is there anything else I should know about the castle? Any secrets it holds?

An innocent question.

Lady Alana's eyes flash dark. "I would stay away from the basement. Nothing good happens there."

"Oh?" I ask casually, despite the sensation of glass sliding down my throat. "What happens in the basement?"

The ladies stare at each other while she shakes her head. Lady Alana presses her lips together. "You are an inquisitive one, aren't you, Ophelia? I will give you a pass because it's your first day. Please know I dislike being questioned like this."

I bow my head and display the mask of obedience I've gotten so good at since I arrived. "Apologies, my lady." My voice remains like honey.

She holds her ugly nose up high. "Very well then. You should probably know anyway. It's where they take the sirens when they catch them. And it's so unfortunate what they must do to them."

My head pounds as heat coils through me, and my vision darkens. It takes every ounce of my willpower not to sing and cut this woman's throat for even speaking of my kind.

Everything I suspected—validated.

I must know if she saw Brielle. "Have you observed what happens down there?" I ask her. My voice is calm—*composed*.

She tilts her head back and laughs. "Oh, heavens no. The king won't reveal his unpleasant tasks to us ladies. I can see how heavy it weighs on him, though. It must be hard being the king."

The room spins around me as my new thread of power lights up inside me. It's so painful now it feels as if it will explode out of me if I don't contain it. She goes on about how terrible my kind is, repeating the same old story we've heard countless times before. How the sirens stole magic from the Throdos family and started an ancient war. Now, they must eradicate all of my species lest we doom humanity.

Lady Alana spews her lies, and I focus my gaze on a pretty glass vase etched in stunning coral sitting on her table. My nostrils flare as the power bundles up inside and explodes out of me. With a jerk of my chin, I send the pretty vase exploding into the wall across the room. It shatters into a million pieces from the force of my rage.

The ladies jump from the glass carnage on the floor and stare at each other confused and frightened, while the blood drains from my face at the realization of what I did.

Lady Alana's eyes grow wide. Her pupils blacken like a raven. "What in Poseidon's name was that?" she cries, as she jumps to her feet and glares at each of her ladies. "Who did that?"

I sit stunned and silent, and they all look at each other. Since I was sitting in the middle of them, no one looks at me.

Bash's dormant power.

No wonder I'm so smitten with him—drawn to him. It's like my blood knew what my mind didn't. The strength he gave me is undeniable.

Lady Alana ignores me, but she seizes Lady Lillian by the collar. Lady Lillian is sitting closest to the glass and shaking like a pitiful leaf. I sit with my back straight, and my muscles grow weak and numb. They would harm me if they knew it was me. A cold shudder runs through me at what they would do.

"It was you, wasn't it Lillian?" she screams at the girl. "Get out of my sight."

Lillian scuttles away in a mighty fright.

"Everyone GET OUT," Lady Alana screams. "I want to have a nap. Bring someone to clean this glass immediately."

A few housemaids come rushing in.

I'm eager to leave this room. While Bash thinks I'm busy with Lady Alana, it's the perfect time to sneak away and explore the castle lands on my own. Plus, I'm in desperate need of a swim. My siren's begging to get out.

I must take some space to think away from Bash's ominous presence and master this new power coursing through my bones and uncover why Lady Alana falsely claims Bash is the true king.

Chapter Seven

OPHELIA

With Lady Alana's lunch cut short from her tantrum and her ladies scattered out, I use the opportunity to slip outside. It's an unseasonably hot mid-summer day, and I'm wearing my favorite opal dress. The only other dress I own other than my fancy gown. It's soft, simple, and allows the wind of the ocean to flow through me, and it reminds me of Brielle. It's one possession of hers I kept after selling all the trinkets when my father died a week ago. The scent of her perfume still lingers on its threads.

My sister and I used to sleep on the beach under the open stars, and once Papa was asleep in his carriage, we slipped into the water to play and our magic would power us. We felt as if we had slept the entire night after returning to land.

Then we'd spend the day selling and swindling various gems, linens, lotions, potions, fabrics, spices, and whatever other delicacies we could sell or steal from people. The streets kept me cunning—*strong*. The dark alleyways of this city make this castle seem like child's play.

I instantly relax as the sea breeze hits my skin, and I make my way down the stone stairs, over the drawbridge and to the rocky beach below.

One night—it took one night for the castle to change me. Today I woke up stronger.

The beach is empty this far below—just the waves and the foamy sea that crashes into the large mosaic of jagged rocks at the bottom of the cliff with its relentless power. The salty breeze brushes against my face as I behold the chaos and beauty where my two worlds collide.

This beach is tucked away from the towering castle above. It's not an ideal swim spot for mere humans—but I'm not a mere human and this is perfect.

Before I slip off my dress to jump into the thunderous waters, I pause. The new power within me itches between the threads of my song, and I must practice my control over it.

As the sun blazes high in the sky, I shift my attention to a lone rock the size of my fist. I flick my hand as I did before, willing it to move just as I did in Lady Alana's chambers.

Nothing—not even an inch.

I grind my teeth. I feel the power within me all bundled up inside; it makes my skin crawl and itch. How do I access it? It's harder for me to control than my voice.

I try to use my song. My voice, soft and sweet, flows out of me toward the rock. I sing from the very depth of my soul, throwing all my power at this single stone, stopping only when I realize how silly I must look. I didn't use my voice to move that glass—I did it another way.

Focus, Ophelia.

My Papa's voice.

I continue for about an hour before giving up completely. Did I imagine the whole thing? Perhaps the glass just fell on its own.

My lip curls, and I kick at the rock and curse from the shooting pain up my leg. I then pick it up and hurl it into the ocean. I'm about to jump right in after when a shadow hints in my peripheral. My heart pulses as I shift my gaze to an old man standing on the path a few feet away, observing me.

Goosebumps prickle my skin, as if a thousand little crabs are crawling all over me. What did he see exactly? The withered old man with a toothless, menacing smile. A fisherman, from the looks of it. Not sophisticated enough to be part of the court or the king's royal fleet, so what's he doing on castle grounds?

What does he want?

He points a crooked finger. "Your voice is that of a sea witch."

I scoff. "It is not."

His voice is rough—accusing. "You need to leave Atlantis, witch. Take that cursed voice with you."

My heart lurches, but I hold strong. "I'm not a witch," I snap at him. He has no proof of this. "I am part of His Majesty's court. I am simply a singer and a member of the royal entertainment. The king wouldn't be pleased with how you're speaking to me."

And by king, I mean my king—*Bash.*

He leers at me from afar. "You play a dangerous game, witch. Remaining in the castle means certain death. Leave now before you die."

My chest tightens. "Why do you say that, old man?"

With a pointed finger, he takes a couple of steps forward. "You're the reason this city will fall. Leave before you curse us all."

"No." I spit at him with all my rage. "I will not leave—I am NOT a witch."

"Go," he screams and stumbles closer. A small misstep, enough to tell he doesn't see me. In fact, he is blind as a bloody bat. There is a certain unsettling quality to the way he looks at me. His gaze seems to pierce right through me, rather than focusing on me directly. What's more, his eyes are an eerie shade of white that gives me goosebumps even in this heat.

A seer—only seer's have white eyes.

My fascination gets the best of me, and I take a couple of steps toward him. I circle him, as I've never seen a real seer before. They are nothing but legends. He continues his babble. "You are evil, Ophelia of the Oceanid, true evil."

I gasp—he even knows my name. He pulls out a knife, a jagged one with a golden hilt. Having seen enough treasures in my lifetime, I know this one is valuable. It flashes in the brilliant sun.

He lunges toward me, and despite his lack of sight, he comes at me with the precisions of a scorpion's tail. My palms sweat and bones ache as fear courses through me. My stomach roils for only a moment before the tension builds up inside me like it did in Lady Alana's chambers.

He raises his dagger and flies at me like a fury in the night. The pit in my stomach grows and explodes through my fingers. I throw him back ten feet into the saw-edged rocks a few feet away below the base of the cliff.

His body crumbles over the stones—his bones shatter.

Despite the flurry of power within me, I barely flicked my fingers. But my breath is heavy and I'm in awe as I behold his frail body lying limp over the sharp rocks.

What have I done?

I run over to him, and his blank eyes seem to stare right into my soul. He laughs, a sinister laugh, as if telling himself a joke only he thinks is funny. "You are the one who will bring this city to its knees, Ophelia of the Ocean. I'll reveal your identity to the king."

I swallow as my breath evens, my eyesight clears, and my muscles quiver. This old man will not be uttering this to a single soul. Especially with all the blood seeping out of him.

My voice is cutting—deadly as I behold him. "I am Ophelia of the Ocean," I say. "I am also a daughter and a sister. I only wish to avenge the ones I love. I'm not an evil witch, old man. I'm just a girl."

Even with the gasps of air he takes with his dying breaths, his voice remains even. "They will burn you, Ophelia. Bleed you out and burn you."

Enough.

I grab the golden knife and slit his throat. His blood washes the rocks with a deadly paint of red. His white eyes turn black and as they should. What an evil old man.

I stand back and stare at him, biting the inside of my cheek, unsure of what to do with the lifeless body splayed out in front of me. Someone will surely find it. I gather my anger, which latches onto the thread of power, and I cast it to him, lifting my delicate hands. His body rises and hovers over the jagged rocks. With a flick of my wrist, I whip his body another twenty feet until it slams into the cliff and falls into the whirling sea below. I use my strength to pull water from the nearby bay, creating a large wave to wash away the blood. The water clears and all is as it was before. No sign of the seer or the blood I spilled here today. I turn and face the ocean. A wind—the one I created with the force of my power—blows through my raven hair and I slip off my opal dress.

I let out a huge breath. No one saw me. No one knows the evil act from my moment of pure terror and desperation. My act of justice. I dive headfirst into the bay and swim away before I even transform. My tail—my glorious tail pushes me fast out of the bay and into the ocean beyond. The sea is a celestial spectacle as the current brushes against my skin. A realm of enchantment and colorful beauty. The sun dances in its azure depths, the vibrant hues pulling me forward toward its ethereal beauty and safety.

A better world. Not full of anger, hurt, or greed.

I swim away from the body and blood as quickly as possible, toward my true home and into the depths of the sea. I heed the seer's warning. Atlantis is no place for me. With my new powers, I can start over and begin anew. The possibilities are endless, and I can go anywhere and be anyone I desire. Just not here, not in this place. Even if it means leaving a piece of my sister behind me. I ignore the pulling tug at my heart, not the pull of my sister or my blinding need for revenge, but a new sensation as the thought of leaving Bash plunges a knife into my heart.

My body suddenly slams into an invisible wall, and I am pushed back a foot from the force of the collision. My eyes widen as I lift my hands and swim in front of the barrier blocking me. The barrier casts an invisible hum around my fingers as I spread my hands upon it.

The wards of the castle—built as an ancient weapon to protect it.

A prison for those like me.

Pearl Castle will not let me leave.

Chapter Eight

BASH

I left Ophelia this morning simply out of a need to maintain my appearance at court. I wanted nothing more than to stay in bed with her, feed her sweet things, and fuck her until there is nothing left of her, ripping at her hair and tugging at her throat while I'm at it. I don't usually pry myself away from women, but I had to with her.

Ophelia is mysterious—the water torture is my usual test to see if they can handle the type of pain I like to give. It's not merely whips and chains, although I enjoy those immensely, but taking them to the edge of death.

It's an art of torture I save for the ones who I really like, and Ophelia passed my test with flying colors. Even after I nearly killed her, her pussy was still wet and throbbing for me. This one has a hold on me—I can't put my finger on why. Other than her luscious silk hair, her tiny waist, suckable tits, and her heavenly pussy.

Unlike the ladies of the castle, Ophelia seems to love the submission, and I can dominate her to my fullest extent, unleash my fury, and show her parts of myself I usually contain. It's rare for a woman to get the full Bash, but in the short time I've known her, Ophelia has peeled back my layers. Her pull on me is strong. Sex with Ophelia will be my undoing.

After dinner, I lounge on the circular, lavish chairs in my usual spot at the edge of the dining hall. This is where we usually go to have our after-dinner drink, where the ladies of court fawn at our feet, and we enjoy our evening entertainment.

Tonight, Alex and Ayden are stuck with the ugly sisters. The Duke and Alex are in an intense conversation about the city's unrest and the army of Dunehaven. Alex's eyes are tight—his golden hair is slicked back beneath his crown. Tonight, he looks . . . stressed. Travelers say this ruler, this Sultan, has seven palaces made of sand instead of stone. As if that's even possible. He also has an army five times the size of ours. Alex is sufficiently distracted with the Duke right now and oblivious to Ophelia's absence.

The usual musician plays a flute, and guests are milling about in the main dining hall. I've not seen Ophelia all day since I left her in my room. Atticus informed me he left her in Lady Alana's chambers, and after an incident, the ladies scattered and Ophelia disappeared.

Perhaps I scared her off more than I thought. Or did Lady Alana get to her? I know she's banned her ladies from seeing me, and to no avail. They often sneak into my chambers, anyway.

Atticus looks for Ophelia, who must be nearby. Either way, she disobeyed me, and I dislike insubordination, so now hot rage circulates through every single vein.

Ayden chuckles as he watches me with his skinny lady Deirdre beside him. A nudge agitates my side. "What's wrong, Bash?" Ayden whispers in my ear, as my anger seeps through my pours. "Trouble with the misses already?"

He knows me too well; we spent too much time together growing up.

My jaw flexes and I grab Lady Lillian, who's sitting next to me on the couch. I pull her onto my lap, rubbing my hand up and down her arm and tickling her thigh.

"Not at all, cousin. The women at court are looking delectable tonight."

Lady Lillian is quite an attractive blonde and does look rather nice with her breasts peeking out of her dress. However, she is not what I desire at the moment. She's favored by the future queen, so I must be gentle with her in bed and find her a boring fuck.

She's not seen my dark side as Ophelia has, or the few of the maids within the castle who like it particularly rough.

Ayden chuckles, "That good, is she?" He laughs loudly, causing other members of the court to stare. He doesn't believe a word I say.

I pointedly ignore him, while Alex leans over with annoyance that runs along his angular face. "Will you two behave tonight? You are causing a scene," he says.

Ayden chuckles. "Sorry, brother."

I lean in and whisper sweet nothings in Lillian's ear, rousing her up. She wraps her arms around my neck and casts looks of defiance to Lady Alana, who's sitting stiff as a board next to Alex. I dare Lady Alana to say something. I will never see her as queen consort. I refuse to bow to her—I shouldn't have to bow to anyone.

I will fuck anyone I want in this court.

Ophelia enters the room a few minutes later. I try to contain my excitement as I admire her with her midnight hair pulled back in ringlets that accentuate her cheekbones, and her cherry lips seem to pop against the subtle color of her elegant dress. Lillian feels my hardening cock and sinks her hips lower into me and giggles, nestling her chin into my neck.

Ophelia casts a single look in my direction. Her eyes flash as she sees Lady Lillian on my lap. Straightening her back and shifting her gaze, she steps onto the stage, embodying the essence of a goddess. She looks different tonight—a confidence she didn't have yesterday.

A glow.

Rage continues its relentless pulse within me. Ophelia ignores me when I should be her entire world. I try not to look distracted by her as Alex watches me from his side of the couch. Alexander would take Ophelia just to spite me if he knew how much I desired her.

She takes her place and captivates the room with her voice. Her eyes graze back to me, and I pull my arms around Lady Lillian and nibble on her ear. Lady Lillian is all too happy to have my full attention right now, and it has the desired effect as Ophelia finally pierces me with her emerald eyes.

She sways her delectable hips and sings, and despite the woman on my lap—my entire world is on the raven-haired woman before me. I envision all the things I plan to do to her later. My hands will rip her apart, while my tongue and cock will please and tease.

My desire, lust, love, and hunger for this woman is like a trance—a prison while she sings, and it drives my cock wild.

It's only on her final song I finally feel it. A whisper—a tingle.

A sliver of magic.

It catches my attention.

Where did it come from? I've not felt it before, and it wasn't here yesterday. I look at Ayden, who seems lost in a trance as Ophelia sings. King Alexander is the sole person in the room with clear eyes but is oblivious to what's happening.

Ophelia's voice—how did I not notice before?

It's magic.

I twist my gaze at her, watching her bewitch the entire room. That simply isn't possible. Only sirens have magical voices, and Ophelia is certainly not a fish. The pussy I fucked last night was most definitely human.

But my talisman doesn't lie. On the surface, it looks like a tiny metal rod barely bigger than the length of my finger. In reality, it's one of the most powerful objects in the entire kingdom. It can detect and steal any magic originated from the Coral Throne. It was a present from my father, to protect me from those who wish me harm. A magical object only meant for the true king, and Alex has no clue of its existence or that I carry it with me constantly. It vibrates in my pocket.

It screams at me.

So how? How does she possess the power of the ocean realm? Of the witches of the sea who seek to destroy us?

Ophelia finishes and the vibrations linger. The room returns, as it was before. Everyone is completely unaware of the magic that just consumed them, and the flute carries on. Amid the music, men approach and ask her to dance, which she gleefully accepts.

Atticus, who is lurking somewhere among the shadows, comes to my side and pours me some more wine as I watch Ophelia in the arms of another man. She stares at him and smiles through those alluring lashes. He places his hands on her hips while they cavort around the dancefloor unaware I plan to kill him for touching those juicy hips which only belong to me.

She's caught the attention of the royal brothers as well. Both golden hair men in their crowns now staring at her as she whips, twirls, and smiles.

An otherworldly luminescence fills the air around her.

Both royals are careful not to look too closely, but even in the dim candlelit hall, their lustful intent is set on their faces. I'll share her with Ayden and need to be cautious to uncover the truth behind her voice. Why did I suddenly feel these vibrations in my pocket?

Over the music, a loud cry echoes from outside in the hall. Ophelia cuts her gaze directly to me as the room grows silent as a castle fisherman rushes in. "The seer is dead," he screams. "Someone killed the seer!" The fisherman rushes up to the king and bows at his feet. Alex merely nods, and the man looks up with pleading eyes. "Sire, someone killed Fredrick. They slit his throat and threw his body into the sea. He was found by my men while fishing near the castle."

My eyes narrow, but I suppress a tingle of joy. Fredrick was Alex's mystical seer, and frankly, he creeped the fuck out of me. I hated him—he once told me I was meant to die a watery death. The worst way to die, if you ask me.

Nevertheless, Fredrick was a castle legend. He roamed the shores of Atlantis, babbling about mystical and seafaring things. Like Atticus, he is always there, coming and going as he pleases. No one knows his true age or how he came to be.

The whole court bursts into chatter. A murder in the castle isn't something to take lightly. Even if it was at the hands of a scoundrel from the city, how did they get through the castle walls? The power of the Coral Throne has wards on these lands. No one can do harm here or come here uninvited. It was someone who was already here. A twinge hits my cock as I think of the midnight beauty that awaits me. It was Ophelia—it must be.

What naughty things were you up to this afternoon, little girl?

The Duke rises. "What is the meaning of this?"

Alex stands and addresses his people with his eyes wide and sweat on his brow, and I suppress the smirk teasing my face. Oh, to be the king.

This is hilarious.

"Sit down, everyone. I will not have disruption at my court." Alex bellows out in his *I am the king so you must listen* voice. He looks at me urgently. "Bash, I need you."

I roll my eyes and annoyance tightens my gut. I've played this role before. The Royal Adviser needs to advise—or, in this case, solve the puzzle. Alex kicks everyone out, so the night is ending early, it seems.

I search for Ophelia, who has disappeared during the chaos. I push Lady Lillian off me. If I can't find Ophelia tonight, I will come find Lillian and rage-fuck her mouth till she's raw and full of my cum. We will see if she still wishes to wiggle on my cock tomorrow night. Or perhaps I will go find the maid slut—she always likes it rough. But those are only secondary options.

I jerk my chin at Atticus, who waits in the shadows like an obedient fool. They know what I want—they know who I want.

Everyone leaves, and now it's only Alex, Ayden, and I sitting on the couch with the castle fisherman trembling at our feet. Quite pathetic, as this man once hooked a siren and lived to tell us about it. He even brought her into our underground water prison we use to slay them. I tolerated his gloating for weeks at court, and now I sit through all the gory details of what Ophelia did with his body while he whimpers like a little girl. He tells us the state Fredrick was in and I am . . . fascinated.

How did she manage it? The tiny wisp of a girl.

"It must be a pirate." Alex decides after contemplating for all of five minutes. "It's the only thing that makes sense. He said something wrong to someone. Unless . . ." He looks at me as shaken and scared as the fisherman. "You think it's the threat from the south?"

I merely nod. "Indeed, you are right your highness. Fredrick had a big mouth. It was only a matter of time before he was gutted."

Alex shakes his head, visibly relieved from my assessment. He struggles with conflict, so this will have him stressed out and distracted.

After another hour of deliberating, Alex finally calls the meeting. I'm dying from boredom, and my knee shakes with anticipation. Atticus finally emerges from the hall, and the twins nod in unison, signaling they were successful in their mission of retrieving Ophelia.

I am no fool. The only recent change in the castle is the girl's presence. Even if I invited her here to begin with, believing in coincidences gets you killed and makes you a weak king.

I rise and stretch, but I give a nod to Ayden to join me before he disappears to his chambers. I must confirm my suspicions about Ophelia and find out what really happened to poor Fredrick.

Chapter Nine

OPHELIA

This castle imprisoned me—these ancient barriers must have trapped me when I stepped foot inside these walls and used my magic. The Coral Throne recognized me and keeps me here. I have no choice but to stay and finish what I started for Brielle. At least now, though, I'm with additional defenses should I need them.

After I crashed into the invisible wall hidden deep within the sea, I slipped onto dry land and back into my clothes. I spent the rest of the day and evening practicing my new skill and primping myself for tonight's dinner. I avoid Bash and his offer to spend the afternoon with me. Bash can wait—I must keep a low profile in case anyone saw what I did to that seer.

Anger fuels Bash's power. That is how I invoked it. It must be his dominant emotion. I am now confident in my ability to move things with my mind, thanks to the abundance of anger that lives within me. Anything as large as a boulder to a tiny kernel of sand.

All the elements—air, earth, and water are also within my control. I've not yet played with fire, yet I know I could make this city burn. My power could destroy this castle and sink it to the darkest depths of the sea. If only Bash knew the power that lies within him. If this tiny sliver makes me this strong, I shudder at what Bash could do if he accessed it.

In the meantime, I could bring Bash to his knees if I wanted to. Instead, I wish to continue playing his little game and bend over for him. Have him punish me with those devilish hands. Then he can help get me in the beds of his royal cousins so I can suck powers out of them, too.

It took all my control not to throw Lady Lillian off his lap and slam her delicate little body into the wall. Bash is toying with me, and I don't like it. I want all his attention, but two can play this deadly game. The other gentleman was a marvelous dancer with strong hands, too. Bash couldn't rip his eyes away from me as he hugged me close on the dance floor, rubbing himself all over me. Bash doesn't fool me—his hands and lips may have been on Lady Lillian's silky skin, but it was me he was watching the entire time.

I'm who he desires.

After the announcement of the seer's untimely death, it didn't take long for Atticus to come collect me from my rooms. I didn't wish to stay around and hear all the gory details of what I did to him, so I slipped away during the chaos.

Atticus is rather rough with me when he barges into my room and tells me Bash has summoned me. That tells what type of mood Bash must be in, and I welcome Bash's bad mood—the angrier, the better.

I suppress the urge to snap Atticus's neck with a flick of my finger as they put their vile hands on me and drag me to the pool room. Bash's preferred room for fucking and breaking women, it seems.

They open the door and push me to the floor. I land with a thud on my hands and knees and strands of hair fall in front of my face. I snap my head up like a sphinx as Bash stares down at me and all my anger melts away. I'm breathless—he's shirtless, standing by the pool. His unearthly body shines in the moonlight, and his dark gaze pierces through me.

I'm infatuated with him. The way he holds himself, his allure, his confidence, how he drips sex. He's the prettiest man I've ever laid eyes on. With his dark hair and ocean eyes, I will take every ounce of pain he can give me if it means I get all his attention tonight.

He flicks his head up and flashes me a smile. "You've been busy, Ophelia." His voice is taunting, and it sends my pussy into a spiral.

I open my mouth to answer him.

"Ah, ah, ah." He cocks his head, and I snap my mouth shut immediately. He glances at the twins, who wait for an invitation to stay. I don't want them watching. He must know that.

Bash storms me. He gives me no room to breathe as he twists me and presses up against my backside. He pulls my head, and his lips graze my neck. "They stay," he growls. "You were not well-behaved today, Ophelia, were you?" He slides his hand down to my breast and squeezes it hard before tracing his fingers along my collarbone and finally around my neck. "Teasing me like that at dinner." His voice a deadly whisper. "You do not dance with any other man in this castle. Is that clear?"

I swallow—wishing for his hands to move to all the other areas of my body. Instead, his hands squeeze my neck, ceasing my ability to breathe. I choke on air and moisture thickens between my legs. Prince Ayden comes into my view and my pulse quickens. He casually sits on a chair near the pool—watching. The baby-faced royal and his magic cum is here to claim me. His lips are curled into a smirk as he watches me suffer. I'll have to play up the damsel in distress. It seems they like it—and Ayden is my end goal tonight.

Bash grabs my chin and whispers. "You may speak, Ophelia. Tell me the rules are clear."

My eyes narrow and lips quirk, and I tell him what I know will infuriate him. "No, my king, they are not clear."

Now I am teasing him, and I brace myself for impact on what I know is coming. He doesn't hit me like I expect. Instead, his hands slide down my chest and he fondles each of my nipples over my clothes before dragging me toward Ayden.

The baby-faced royal is staring at me with puppy dog eyes, and I finally get a clear view of him. His sandy blond hair is longer than Bash's, but not as long as King Alexander's. He's strong but not as strong as Bash. He's cute and, more importantly—he's royal. I smell the power on him, just like I did with Bash.

King Alexander is the wild card. He seemed unaffected by my voice both times I sang for him. At least, he didn't notice the control I have over his subjects. The Coral Throne's power seems to serve me, not refuse me. Like it's chosen me for something.

Prince Ayden grabs a piece of my fallen hair. "Don't be so hard on her, Bash." He warns. "I don't like them roughed up like you do."

Bash grips my arms. "She should have considered that before using that word. We will have to punish you tonight without bruising your pretty face, won't we, my sweet?"

He pulls my ear to his mouth and jerks his head toward Ayden. "Do you want him, Ophelia? The Prince of Atlantis."

I nod and lean my head back on him, enjoying Bash's warmth. With a forceful grip, he directs my gaze toward the twins with a disgusting gleam in their eyes. "Do you want Atticus, the castle steward?" He laughs.

My stomach twists. I will destroy those vile men before they get their cocks anywhere near me. He then twists me to look at him. "Or is it me you desire, Ophelia slut?"

My chest rises and falls as he presses me close against him. His lips are so close, I can taste the sweet scent of his after-dinner drink on his breath.

It's him—Bash, I want in this moment. He slides his fingers down to my pussy. My wetness leaks as he curves his thumb and fingers deep inside, moving the threads of my panties aside. I moan at the pleasure of it, aware how close Ayden is. I like that he's watching. Maybe if I'm well-behaved, they will take me together.

Bash laughs. "I guess it's me you want, then."

A breathy moan escapes me. "Yes, my king."

My folds wrap tightly around his fingers, and he fondles me before grabbing me around by my waist and elevates me. The threads of power now thrumming, anticipating him as I curl my legs around him while his soft warm hands cup my ass. I lean my head up, grazing my lips on his neck, but I don't dare to kiss him. Not without his permission. He faces me toward the prince, whose tongue slides across his bottom lip.

Bash places me on top of the baby royal, so my legs are straddled along each side of him. We are both fully clothed, but his cock presses firmly against my clit as Brielle's opal dress bunches at the side.

Bash leans over me, his lips tickle my ear. He licks my neck and nips at my ears with his hands now firmly on my waist. "I want you to dance on him, Ophelia. Dance for your prince and dance for me. Make your pussy so wet for me, my sweet."

I arch my back and lean over Prince Ayden but pause when Atticus comes into view, my entire body bristles. I look over at Bash, who merely cocks a knowing brow. "Your punishment, Ophelia," he says, as he runs his hand down the length of my back. "You're fortunate I'm not in a sharing mood and don't let them have their way with you. They will watch everything tonight, though."

My insides tighten, and it takes every ounce of me to control the raging anger that powers me. I won't let Bash know about my powers, even though I could splatter these men against the wall. So, I do my best to ignore them. One day, I plan to make the twins explode from the inside out.

Ayden looks at me with a soft gaze and rubs his fingers over my brow, moving my hair that's fallen over my face. He shifts beneath me, his cock pressing into me. "She's a pretty one, cousin. Prettier than that wretched skinny beast Alex is making me bang."

Bash ripples back to the shadows. "I told you so, Ayden, but this one is mine to keep. You can play with her, but she's off-limits without my approval and never without me."

Ayden snickers as he flicks his tongue along my nipple when I lean forward to tease him with it. "Whatever you say, Bash."

My pussy clenches at Bash calling me his—claiming me even with a higher noble. It's incredibly sexy, and it makes me mad to please him.

I focus on Ayden's deer-like eyes, rolling my body over him as Bash asks me to do. I lift my arms above my head, running my hands through my hair, and I smile at him. He bites his lower lip as if he can't stand the thought of not being inside me and slides his hands up and down my waist, caressing the lines of my back. I plan to give these men the show they've asked for.

But first a kiss—I roll my hips and lean forward, and he meets me with his soft lips. I suck on his tongue and caress his face. He seems to enjoy it as he groans and slips his hands up my dress, pulling it off me completely. I grind on him, pressing down onto the bulge of his pants, which drives him wild as my nipples tighten from the ocean breeze that hits them.

He growls and rips off my mouth, moving his lips to my nipples, biting and sucking on each of them. I keep rolling my hips until the throbbing and heat are too much to bear. I rub my fingers along my clit till my orgasm crests and I let out a soft moan as a tiny one waves through me.

Ayden is . . . cute. His hands are soft, and his tongue is warm as he presses kisses all over me. He's childlike in a lot of ways, although he is of age.

He's eager and playful, and I love how different he is from Bash. I'm curious to see what his power will give me. His cock is so close only a thin layer of his pants separates us. I can almost taste it—the power seeping out of its tip.

Like a dog desperate for a treat, I lean down and begin pulling at his pants. Pain sears my head as Bash pulls my hair back in his iron grip. I meet his deadly eyes as his pupils flair.

"Ophelia. You desperate, greedy little whore," he says with a silky voice. "I didn't say you could touch him like that."

I try to swallow, but his pull is too hard; he has my head yanked back. He grabs me and plucks me off of the prince, gathering me in his arms. Bash is soft again, his hands a caressing embrace as he carries me across the room. I melt into him—completely submitting to whatever he wants me to do. He places me on the ground and stares down at me. I look up at him in a feline position on all fours.

His eyes narrow, and his voice is a threat. "I want you to sing now, Ophelia. A private show just for the four of us."

My muscles tighten. I rarely sing for small groups. I don't know how my power will impact them, but I do as he says, and I rise to stand in front of them. It's clear to me now just how much younger and inexperienced Ayden really is compared to his cousin. Even though he is a prince, Ayden defers to Bash. Bash is the royal in charge.

Like a true king.

Ignoring the twins, I project my voice to the two royals. Soft and sweet, I sing. I know I have them. Their eyes grow wild—ravishing. Like they want to tear me apart. After a few moments, and even though I continue singing, their eyes simmer to their normal state.

A twinge hits my stomach. Something isn't right and a pain so deadly runs through my blood. I drop to the ground as my body grows weak and bones brittle as I feel my power seeping out of me.

My voice—he stole my voice.

Bash stares at me. His eyes perfectly blue and clear. He utters my name. "Ophelia . . ."

The way he says it.

"Ophelia, what was that?"

Despite my shaking body, I muster the courage to look up at

him. I reach for my power, any thread of it I can grasp onto. And it's gone. Nothing but an empty void of darkness rests in its place.

Bash circles me now, his eyes burning into me as if trying to uncover my secret. I have a feeling he already knows. He has something that is suppressing my voice, something that has trapped it. He's wearing the hat of the Royal Adviser now—whatever remnants of my lover suckling on my tits, is gone from his eyes.

I lie in a heap on the ground and wrap my arms around myself. He bends down and rubs his knuckles on my face. "What are you, Ophelia?" He ponders as he takes in my eyes, then draws his attention to my hair and my completely exposed naked body.

I don't answer, partly because I do not know. Sirens don't have the power to move things with their minds. This is unusual—new. Even I know that.

He grabs my chin. "What dirty secrets do you hold, my sweet?"

I open my lips, but nothing comes out, so I bite them in defiance and cross my arms.

A click of his tongue. "I know magic when I see it." He bends down and picks me up like I'm nothing more than a delicate seashell. "And you, little girl, are teeming with magic. I don't know how I didn't see it before. Your voice . . ."

My throat dries up when I notice him holding a rod of some sort. That must have captured my voice and stalled my powers.

He knew—or suspected, at the very least. I was careless.

Stupid and careless.

He drags me over to the pool and hurls me in it. When my legs hit the water, my tail transforms, and my body lengthens. It happens in an instant—my siren form takes over. My beautiful tail shines in the moonlight, casting a glow around it. The four of them peer over the edge, and their eyes grow wide.

Bash made a careless mistake. I'm capable of protecting myself in this form, and I am far from the weak, helpless girl he thought I was. I hiss and whip my tail at him, barely missing his head with its razor-sharp edge. He won't get near me while in my true oceanic form. I'm stronger than him and he knows it. Plus, I still have my other power—he does not know this, so I keep it hidden. He can only take it from me if I use it. At least, that's what I suspect.

Their eyes go from fascination to straight fear as I whip my tail and splash water all over them. I will make sure they always fear me from this moment forward.

No silly rod can deprive me of what I was born with. My tail gives me more power than my voice and telekinesis combined—access to completely different worlds.

I rise in the water and face them, ready to show them what they are dealing with, but something pulls me in—a force below, sucking me down.

The pool is draining, and I am stuck due to the strong water flow pulling me down and the surrounding pressure. If Bash drains the pool, I will be powerless. Nothing but a weak little girl. If I use my other power, he will steal it, too.

I fall through a trapdoor and plummet into darkness until I hit a wall of water deep in the castle. Once I come to my senses, I realize I am still in my siren form. It's dark—a veil of obscurity shrouds my view.

They put me in a prison—a special one, made for beings like me. A place where sirens go to die. I swim around to get a better sense of what I'm dealing with. It's barely more than a pit made of glass, and when I whip my tail against it, it doesn't break.

They use this room to watch us die like vermin—as if we aren't rare and magnificent creatures they should cherish. Sirens should never endure this. Not when we're accustomed to swimming in the vast ocean. The prison's size is more torturous than the darkness that surrounds me. Brielle spent her final days here and I will, too.

I swim a small circle. I swim until a tiny light illuminates my view. I press my face up against the glass as Bash and the others watch me holding a single torch.

I refuse to die here today. Bash will not kill me. I have an advantage over Brielle—a royal who desires me. And tonight, I will show them how powerful sirens really are.

Chapter Ten

BASH

The castle has one simple rule—a single commandment nobody should break under our oath to the Coral Throne. It's one rule Alex holds very dear to all that serve him. An ancient rule passed down for generations as we work to eradicate the species that can destroy us. The rule is clear, and if broken, is grounds for immediate beheading.

Don't fuck a fishy.

Oops.

"What should we do with her?" Ayden asks as he stands beside me, watching Ophelia circle her prison with the focus and precision of a stingray. The hatred in her eyes is clear every time she passes me, and I can't take my eyes off of her in that spellbinding glass prison.

She's simply stunning—majestic and scarier than all the gods.

Her elongated tail, with hints of shimmering greens and hues of purple that seem to morph and change, as if reacting to the thoughts swirling in her brain. Her eyes glow like coral, and her skin is translucent, like soft beach sand.

I shake my head as I behold her. "I don't know, cousin. I've not seen anything like her."

For once, I don't have a smart response. I should tell Alex immediately; a siren is one subject I don't want to push him on. If he finds out I fucked her already, that alone could be grounds for my execution. Every moment that passes where I don't tell him, he will consider treason.

These creatures always terrify me—their power, the hold they have on men. They rule the oceans, rivaled only by the sea itself in its magnificent glory. They say Poseidon made these creatures, built them to serve him. He created a weapon to take over as the supreme power in their divine realms. It ended up as a failed experiment. Even the Gods have lady troubles, it seems. No wonder I'm so infatuated with her. She was seducing me, enchanting me, pulling me into her tangled web of death. I simply didn't know what I was fucking. She felt like any other woman I've been with, a very human pussy indeed.

But I can't bring myself to give her to him yet. He will do what he does with them to regain the power he lost—the power I lost from *my* bloodline.

That makes Ophelia my mortal enemy.

"I don't want to tell Alex about her yet," Ayden whines. And I agree with him. I'm not ready for this pretty creature to bleed out. Plus, I have other suspicions about her I need to confirm.

"It's not fair," Ayden continues in the spoiled voice of a prince used to getting his way, "I didn't even get to fuck her."

I place my hand on his arm and squeeze as Ophelia circles her prison. "Ayden, under no circumstances do we fornicate with a fish—no matter how beautiful they are. She is lethal and will kill you should she have a chance."

He was too young to see the last one, who also had raven hair and beauty like the young woman before me now.

Interesting.

That one was particularly aggressive—stunning but wild. Alex had to kill her quickly.

Ophelia is unlike anything I've ever seen. A siren with two legs and acts so—*human.* If we had removed that siren from the water four years ago, would we have seen legs instead of a tail? Their similarities are too obvious, and I want to kick myself for not seeing it before. Instead, I invited this temptress into this castle and into my bed. She could have killed me in my sleep last night while resting in my arms and I would have been powerless to stop it.

Yet—she didn't and now I am safe, and she is in the depths of this castle where strong and ancient magic ward this prison. Unless Alex specifically knows she is here, he will not come down here.

Like a fury, she whips around the water prison with her long black hair trailing behind her. Her bare breasts tease me as they did last night. And part of me, a bigger part than I'd care to admit, is not done sucking those perfectly full tits—even if she is a fish.

I need to find out more about what she is and her potential. No one can just kill a seer. Fredrick was older than all three of us royals combined. An ancient being—protected by the Coral Throne. Or so I thought. No one knew his origins. He's always just existed.

A creature of the castle.

It would take great power for someone to kill him the way Ophelia did. So, how did she do it? My groin tightens. I must have given her power when I fucked her last night. That is why we hold this ancient rule so dearly. Their methods for stealing our powers have remained unchanged for a millennium.

So, what did she take from me?

I've ensured Atticus's silence about her for now, which buys me a bit of time to figure this out. And Ayden . . . well, Ayden can't keep his eyes off her. I know that look. "Get that idea out of your mind, boy." I warn him. Ayden isn't done with her. His cock still clearly reacting to the lap dance she gave him.

Ayden cuts his spoiled gaze to me. "You got to fuck her. Why can't I?"

I turn him to face me and away from Ophelia, who is now swooping her tail in a circle, causing a cyclone in her prison. A stark reminder of how powerful she is—and how easily she could crush us while in her natural form. A far cry from the tiny girl she was pretending to be.

"She is not human, Ayden," I explain. "And I only fucked her when I thought she was."

"Was it good? I bet she was good."

Stupid boy. He's only thinking with his cock now. We need to be smart about this.

I arch a brow. "That's not the point."

In fact, she was good—

Amazing. Otherworldly. The best sex of my life.

Her tiny pussy was so tight even the thought of it makes me want to explode. The way she submitted to me, so eager to please. A complete opposite of what she is now—a monster, a predator, a master in her own right.

At least I can explain my obsession with her, why I was so drawn to her. My lust is so powerful. It wasn't real. I was cursed by her power when I first saw her sing in the tavern, which resulted in my attraction to her.

Rage circles my insides, clenching my loins. How did I not see it sooner?

She's a siren—the song I thought was that of the gods is nothing more than the song from the sea. And now I have that song trapped. She will never vex another man again.

"You need to go, Ayden. Let me deal with her."

"But . . ."

"Go. Now—if Alex finds out about her, I don't think you will avoid the penalty he must give. I brought her into this castle. I alone need to clean up this mess."

I'm only avoiding the inevitable. Ayden is accustomed to getting his way. He will give me space to think, but I know he will want her to finish his lap dance eventually. And I'll have to appease the twins as well. Their loyalty will only go so far. They will want to have their fun, too.

Ayden leaves, and for at least a day, my secret will be safe. Plus, this will be a good test. Ayden says he's loyal to me, but Alex is his brother. Eventually, I'll give Ayden what he wants.

I'm completely alone, I turn to find Ophelia. I flinch and step back when I behold her. She pressed right into the glass, still as a statue save her hair that flows in the surrounding water. She watches me with an unflinching, lethal gaze. Her azure eyes glow brightly. I flash her a cocky smirk, and she turns and whips her tail at the glass in front of me with a mighty swipe. Even with this pool warded, I can't help but take two steps back. Will the magic even work on a creature like Ophelia? A beautiful freak of nature that defies the laws of reality. One who will kill me the second she has a chance.

We lock eyes, and time seems to stand still as we gaze at each other. Her fiery eyes are captivating, and the thought of having her makes my cock throb. I pull a lever, and the water drains back into the ocean that surrounds this watery pit. When the final drop of water leaves her prison, I marvel as she transforms in front of me. And now she lies helpless, naked, and exposed.

And human.

I'll leave her like this for the night in her weak, brittle form. I need to remind her who holds the power. So tiny, so vulnerable, and the most precious thing I've seen in my life.

Chapter Eleven

BASH

I slept terribly.

I left Ophelia and came back to my room in a rather shitty mood. All night as I lie alone in my bed, I keep smelling her. Her ocean scent mixed with junipers from my soaps lingers on the threads of my silk pillows.

I dozed off thinking of those ruby-red lips wrapped around my cock and how those same lips are pouting downstairs, helpless and completely at my mercy. I grab my growing erection and stroke it as dangerous thoughts swirl in my brain. I've already fucked her—what does it matter if I do it again?

The damage is done.

I dismiss the thought. The risk of Alex finding out isn't worth it. The curse of her power must be having lingering effects and is playing with my mind. Alex would be right to execute me—I'd do the same if I wore the crown and he purposely fucked a siren, knowing they can be my undoing.

But still . . . she's too close to not go and at least play with for a few minutes. I can control myself, and her voice will no longer vex me. I'll keep my talisman close by just in case she tries anything I'm not expecting. This is my only chance to be with her alone. Ayden will want to see her again soon, especially knowing I've already had her. I saw it in his eyes before he left. That spoiled boy is barely a man.

I rise from my bed and slip on my silk robe, ignoring my tussled hair. I don't look as composed as I usually do when I leave my chambers, but Ophelia has already seen all I offer. So, I go relaxed, true to my nature as she is to hers.

When I arrive, she is how I left her, still crumpled in a ball on the stone floor of the now dried up watery prison where we usually keep beings like her.

I haven't been here since we caught the last one. I hope I can stop Ophelia from suffering a similar fate. Her death was unfortunate. Alex really had a temper that day. Her screams were so loud I heard them from above—the whole castle did.

I'll bet my life that siren is the exact reason Ophelia is here.

I open the trap doors to Ophelia's prison and stand over her. I'm not worried about her hurting me. Right now, she is a mere girl who risked everything to come here. I simply wish to learn a bit more about her.

The only tiny movement she gives me is a flash of her eyes through her long lashes as she gazes up at me. I bend down and gather her in my arms. To my surprise, she doesn't give me a fight. She melts into me as I carry her up the ladder and into the room above; a dreadful chamber made of stone.

So, I sneak her to my bedroom. I use the back way, the hidden tunnels within the castle that lead to my closet. I carry her delicate body and take her through the inner walls I know so well. These series of hidden chambers and tunnels have proved useful over the years, and I've taken great care to keep them a secret. Only my father knew of them and his father before that. Now only I know of their existence.

I place Ophelia on my bed once we reach the safety of my room. I ignore the twitch in my cock at the sight of her naked. Only one night ago, I fucked her guilt free—and now she's forbidden to me. And we all know how much I enjoy following rules.

The skin on her neck has tiny bruises, beautiful shades of violet, from my attempt to drown her. I chuckle as I stand at the end of the bed—watching her. "What a performance, Ophelia. You had me fooled last night. You could breathe that entire time, couldn't you? Not the little damsel in distress you pretend to be, are you?"

Water torture breaks them quicker. It helps me train them. But I wasn't training her—she was training me that entire time.

Simply spectacular.

I get nothing. No response, no movement, just a shiver from where the ocean breeze from my open windows hits her silky skin. That and her piercing gaze of hatred and contempt.

I rise and grab a blanket and walk over to her. I can't take my eyes off her for even a second. I've simply never seen a siren with legs before. If I hadn't seen her tail with my own eyes, I never would have believed it. She is what dreams are made of. Her long black hair dances off her ivory skin. She is possibly the most beautiful creature I have ever seen.

"Would you like me to warm you up, Ophelia, my sweet?" I ask her, holding the blanket up.

The snarl on her lips is as vicious as the venom in her eyes.

I know she can't speak. Her voice is within my control. But her supple nipples tighten. Her body responds to my voice, even if she doesn't want it. That is my superpower—my hold on women. Perhaps my training these last couple of days wasn't for nothing after all.

I slide up on the bed as she crawls away from me and rests her head against my headboard, watching me with those sultry eyes. The sight of her bare legs smooth against the dark sheets is . . . *fascinating*. I can't help myself; I must explore her.

I kneel in front of her and open the palm of my hand and she flinches.

"Now now . . . my sweet. I won't hurt you. No punishment tonight, at least not physically. I think you've been punished enough." I let out a little chuckle. "Unfortunately, given what you are, the pain you will experience in this castle is far from over."

She cocks her head, but she doesn't stop me as I open her legs and run my hand down the inside of her thigh. Her human, gorgeous, firm, long, luscious, ivory legs. And her tight, juicy little pussy. All very womanly—just exquisite. I am aware of her exceptional ability to use both her legs and her vagina. She wrapped herself around me last night as I rammed my cock so hard inside her.

I shake my head. *I fucked a fish.* I'll make sure it doesn't happen again. I can't do it twice knowing what she is and what her kind is capable of. I am a Throdos and the true king—she is my mortal enemy.

My eyes find hers. "You wish to hurt me right now, don't you, Ophelia?"

A pause and a nod.

I smile but suppress the rage boiled up inside me. "That does not make me thrilled. And here I thought you wanted to make me happy."

She opens her mouth to speak, but no voice comes out. She grabs her neck as if remembering again her vexing magic sits within my control. One flick of my wrist and I can give it back to the throne. It will be over. Fortunately for Ophelia, that is not what's most valuable to us. Her blood matters most, the very essence of her being. Alex would kill for a single drop of it.

It's all rather . . . *unfortunate*. They really are glorious creatures. I've always had a fascination with them.

Vicious. Cunning. Mesmerizing.

I lie beside her and pull the blanket up over us. She turns to face me, her emerald eyes blazing. I'm dying to know what she has to say, but I can't risk it. She may gain the upper hand if she sings, and I want her to belong to me.

"Do you want your voice back, Ophelia?"

A loaded question. She was born with the power, though it wasn't meant to be hers.

Her cherry lips part, and her body is like ice beside me. I pull her in close to me as I simply cannot have a shivering girl in my bed, sea creature or otherwise. I press my lips to her ear. "What will you do for me if I promise to give it to you?" I murmur.

She licks her lips and my cock springs to life. She keeps her translucent eyes on me as I nudge her head downward underneath the sheets where it's nice and warm. I pull my cock out and press it to her face.

To my delight, she wraps her mouth around it, her tongue flicking the end as she sucks and pulls and takes it deep in her throat. I moan and flinch and grab onto the sides of my bed to steady myself, as she licks and plays with the tip and sucks me hard, deep, and fast.

It doesn't take me long till I explode inside her mouth.

It's the best blow job of my life. I felt her hatred in every single suck, and I want more. My cock bursts back to life at the thought of being with her all night alone.

The rule only states I can't have sex with a siren. No one ever said anything about this. This is way too much fun. I think I will cancel all my appointments tomorrow and spend the entire day with her instead.

I can keep her here like this, my silent, pretty girl. No one will know or hear her scream when she doesn't even have a voice. All I have to do is share her once in a while with Atticus and Ayden. She will be safest with me than anywhere else in the castle.

She pulls her head up beneath the sheet and wipes her mouth clean from my cum spilling out of her mouth. Her translucent eyes glow like the depths of the ocean, and I'm instantly reminded of what she is. It's the same shimmering glow as her tail. A smile forms on my lips as I run my hands through her hair and caress her soft skin. I won't stick my cock inside her tonight, but I do plan on putting my mouth on every single inch of her body before the night is done.

Chapter Twelve

OPHELIA

I awaken to Bash staring down at me through his dark blue eyes and a tight smirk on his lips. His hair falls in little wisps, shining in the early morning light cascading across the room. The bed smells like me—my juices he made flow out of me all night long. And it smells like him—manly and powerful.

He's smiling as he caresses my forehead and presses his lips to my brow. He wraps his arms around me in a warm embrace. "Good morning, Ophelia." His silky voice is like chocolate.

I don't know what came over me last night. While humiliated and trapped in prison, I came up with various fun ways to kill Bash. I thought of flinging him into the ocean and severing his body on those same jagged rocks as that dreadful seer. Explode him from the inside as I plan to do with Atticus. Experimenting with his limbs would also be enjoyable. Twist and contort them into all sorts of fun poses or torture him until he gives me my voice back. The poor soul is unaware of the true extent of my power, what I took from him, or my precise abilities.

But when he came for me as I knew he would and stuck his cock in my face, I simply wanted to please him, pleasure him, make *him* feel good, and give him everything he desired. I had no control . . .

I may wish to keep him, even if it means going against everything I stand for. But I can't forget what he's taken from me. *Who he's taken from me . . .*

I stare back at him with my face like stone, the pain and sorrow radiating from my eyes as my heartbreak for Brielle seeps into every bone.

Bash's voice is soft, caring. "Are you hungry?" he asks with a gleam in his eye. "Do fishes even eat?"

There is no malice in his voice, so I merely cock one eyebrow and glare at him as he watches me with amusement. A snicker sneaks out of him. "I'm just teasing, my sweet. I will send for some breakfast. I don't plan on letting you leave this room today. I think it's time you and I had a little chat."

I tilt my chin and lower my eyes. Not a funny joke, as he will be the only one doing any talking.

He chews on his lip. "If I were to give you your voice back. Do you promise not to use it on me?"

I nod my head three times. Even if I wanted to, that silly iron rod is firmly within his control, and I've felt what it can do and the power that *thing* has over me.

He sighs and rolls on top of me, pressing his hard body into mine. "How do I know I can trust you, Ophelia? You have, after all, been lying to me since the moment we met."

He rubs his hand along my breasts, wrapping his mouth around my nipple. I arch my back and lick my lips, wanting more of him.

He spent the entire night kissing, licking, and nibbling me. For someone who won't fuck a fishy, he sure loves the taste of one.

"Did you enjoy what I did to you last night, Ophelia?" He stares up at me while he nips and runs his teeth along my flesh.

He means what he did with his tongue.

I nod my head three times more as his erection pulses into my thigh. He bears his head into my belly, kissing me until I squirm. "Do you want me to do it again?" He murmurs, and his eyes shimmer. I bite my lip as slickness forms between my thighs at the thought of it.

I shouldn't want this man who bears the last name of those who wish me harm. He watched Brielle die or even killed her himself. But I desire him—my body aches for him.

I turn my head as a bang echoes from the front of the room and the baby-faced prince walks in. The hum of my energy ignites, almost as though sensing and craving its other half, which runs through the blood of this boy. Ayden's eyes widen when he sees me lying naked in Bash's bed, with Bash lying on top of me. The tip of his erection now playing at my entrance, now dripping and aching for him.

The blond prince is the reason I spared Bash's life and why I was so willing with him last night. *Royal cum.* I need to find out what power Ayden will give me.

A sly smile forms on the prince's lips as he beholds me. "I knew it, Bash. I knew you'd have her in here. You're fucking her, aren't you? Why wouldn't you wait for me?"

Bash sighs and rolls off me, carefully pulling the blanket over me. "I assure you, cousin, I am not fucking her."

I clench my jaw at the reminder he seems to not want me like that anymore, now that he knows what I really am.

Ayden whines. "I want my turn with her. And it sure looks to me like you're fucking her."

Bash simply smiles at him, then at me. "We were playing, that is all. Weren't we, Ophelia?"

Ayden takes a few steps forward, peering at me. "I went to see her, but she wasn't there." He shakes his head, and his bright eyes graze me. Heat twinkles within them. "You're playing with fire, Bash. When Alex finds out what you did, he will be furious."

Bash eyes his cousin with one arching brow. "You mean what we did, cousin?" He slides the blanket down, exposing my naked body. "If you want her, dear prince, she is all yours. I kept her warm for you."

Bash looks at me, his fingers graze my cheek and he nods. He's giving me permission—finally. I expected to do this the hard way.

Another click of the door and the twins emerge while a tightness forms in my chest. Of course, Atticus would come, too. They are Bash's little pets. I'm curious about their usefulness to him beyond being creepy. I should kill them and be done with it.

But I can't. It will expose my gifts, then Bash will steal them with his steel rod. Then he will throw me back in that prison pool and I can never avenge my sister.

I must be patient. Bash can't know how much they sicken me.

Bash yanks my hair once more—the darker side of him showing through. His iron grip is harder than I've yet to experience. He pulls me up and out of bed and places his mouth to my chin—licking it. "You will finish what you started for the royal prince, fishy slut." He gathers me in his arms and throws me on the baby-faced prince, who is now lounging on Bash's couch with his hands above his head. I land on Ayden's lap and wrap my legs around him in a straddle. I stare wide eyed at Bash parting my lips, reminding him this could be him next.

He clicks his tongue and shakes his head. "Oh no, you little fishy whore. You don't get to have me. I don't fuck fish."

He just kisses them and licks their insides, but who's paying attention?

Ayden shifts beneath me. Finally, I will get what I need from him. Then, I'll have no excuse not to kill both of them. If I'm fast enough, I can escape before Bash even realizes what I did. Bash will be the first I kill if he lets Atticus watch me like we are in some sleazy brothel. Which he does. The twins stand on either side of the couch, getting a better view as Ayden pulls out his cock and circles my hole with it. He teases and rubs it, pressing his tip just inside as I grind and roll my body over him, doing my best to ignore their sickening presence.

Ayden laughs. "Don't worry, fish. You will have your turn with them after I'm done with you. We've all come for you today."

I give Bash a pleading look.

Bash steps forward. "The twins leave. Ophelia is just for us, Ayden. They can't get involved."

Ayden brushes him off. "But they love watching. It's why they are so loyal to us, Bash."

Bash shakes his head. "Not today. She's gone through enough, and she has to endure much more."

Ayden rolls his eyes. "Fine. Whatever you say." The twins disappear into the shadows just as he grabs my waist and penetrates me without warning. "You're getting soft, cousin." He grunts as I slide my pussy deep over him. "She's that good, eh?"

Bash cuts his gaze to the twins just before they leave. "Don't tell Alex yet. You'll both have a turn, but not today. The prince and I have some matters to attend with her."

They bow in unison. "Yes, your Grace."

Relieved they are gone, I arch my back and I pick up my pace, squeezing my pussy in ways I've not thought possible, all to get the prince's cum inside me.

"Fuck," he cries out, as he meets my thrusts with equal amounts of enthusiasm. "I can see why you like this one, Bash. Are all sirens so tight and eager?"

Bash merely snickers as he watches from the side. "I wouldn't know, cousin. Fornicating with one knowingly is treason."

Ayden doesn't seem to care as he turns me over and fucks me from behind, gripping my hips and thrusting deep as I lay on all fours.

It's small at first, but I feel the power of him sliding into my bones. The same tingle as earlier with Bash. A sliver, a tiny kernel—but that's all I need. It grows within me. I felt it then and I feel it now and I know it's mine forever. I open my mouth in a silent moan, not from Ayden's cock drilling me hard, but from the power within him planting its seed.

Ayden pulls out, then leans over and whispers, "I like to do it in every hole. Be a good slut and arch your back so I can enter your ass."

His attempts at domination are adorable. To match Bash's skill, this boy has a lot to learn. My eyes find Bash, and he gives me a nod, and I do what he says. I gasp for only a second as he penetrates me. It hurts a little, but I can handle the pain. An entirely new sensation and I wish it was Bash exploring me, not Ayden. He doesn't last long before flipping me and exploding all over my belly.

He lets out a ragged breath as he finishes, then turns to his cousin and smiles. "The mutant's all yours again, Bash. I have to get back to Deirdre. She makes me have tea with her in the morning."

I had all but forgotten Ayden is engaged. I am content to see him go back to his ugly betrothed and hope he thinks about me while he is gone. I got what I needed from him, after all.

Ayden snickers as he pulls his cock back in his pants and stares at his cousin. "There, now we've both done it. Alex won't kill both of us. But you should tell him soon. Atticus will slip up, especially if you keep sending them away like that. He requested a meeting with you after breakfast to address the Fredrick situation."

As quickly as Ayden came, he disappears again. It's just me and Bash once more. Except it's not—a new entity lingers, and it's growing by the second. I smile as I lie back on the couch and spread my legs, letting my dark hair flow over my chest—daring, teasing, taunting him as my new power threads with my old.

Bash sits at the end of his bed and leers at me while I wither from the pleasure of it. But to my dismay, he dresses himself, walks over to me, and leans down to press a kiss to my brow. Then grabs my hair and pulls me up to him. "Stay here, my sweet," he whispers. "I'll return to you shortly. If I don't appear at breakfast, Alex will get suspicious."

He gestures toward the balcony and lets out a coy smile. "Help yourself to a bath if you wish. Clean yourself up for me, Ophelia. Spread your gorgeous fins. I'll be back to collect you soon."

Chapter Thirteen

OPHELIA

I slept for a bit after Bash left. I had no way of leaving his rooms. Warded—the entirety of them. His balcony is much too high in the castle for me to jump off. I would fall to a blundering death below.

I bathed, of course, stretching out my tail as much as I could in Bash's gilded tub and stared out to the glistening sea that serves as my beacon. Once finished and satisfied with my siren, I primped and prepped using Bash's lotions and powders and slipped on one of his tunics since he left me completely nude.

Now the newest thread of power vibrates within me, and I ready myself to master it, as I did with the other. I have no idea what this power is or what emotion I must invoke to fuel it.

With the telekinesis it was easy. I willed that glass vase across the room with my anger and shattered it as I intended. This one is a mystery that's vexed me all morning. The power is festering inside me, waiting to come out. It heats the pools of my belly.

So, what is it?

I grip my fists and center myself in the center of the room, deciding to practice my other power instead. I carefully pick up and place down Bash's things with such precision. Little windstorms form by my hands, and I shove them down to the lower levels of the castle, where others are trying to enjoy their morning tea with sunshine and seafaring views. It's nice to know I possess the power that could wash away the ocean.

I gaze at the sea for hours until I have a sudden urge to control the enormous body of water sprawled out in front of me. I'm curious about the size of the waves I can make from up here. Test my abilities—forge my strength.

I am so lost in my thoughts I don't hear Bash come in as he slides his hands up behind me, playing and tugging at the hem of my tunic right above my lady parts. His mouth is so close to my cheeks, the heat of his body ignites me.

"It looks good on you, my sweet." Bash kisses my earlobe. His warm hands wrap around my bare stomach as he lifts my shirt. I take in his delicious scent, but bristle at his touch.

Was Brielle treated the same way when they discovered her years ago? Somehow, I doubt it. They locked her up in the prison pool in the bowels of this castle, lonely and in despair. Bash didn't dominate her, then love and grope her as he is doing with me.

She was in her siren form when they found her. They would have had no reason to suspect her ability to walk on dry land among the humans that hunt her. The thought of Brielle rolling in her watery grave sickens me most of all.

I've been a bad sister—she would be more than disappointed in me. Fucking my captors, knowing what they did to her and sucking off Bash for the mere enjoyment of it.

This needs to stop now—these royals must die before they destroy me. I have to start with Bash. I'm the weakest when it comes to him.

I snap my head up at him, resting and angling it against his muscular chest. My jaw clenches, and I shoot him a deathly glare while anger seeps out of my eyes.

His pupils flare, and he grabs me by the chin. "Come now, Ophelia. It's not that bad here with me, is it? I have simple rules you need to follow, and I will always treat you like the queen you are. I could keep you locked in this room. Imagine the fun we would have." He arches a brow as he rubs his hands along my sides. "I do love seeing you in my clothes. Why don't we lie down and spend the rest of the day in bed?" He gestures to a tray of breakfast pastries and juices he must have brought in with him. "I brought you an array of treats."

I frown and shake my head. Then I mouth the word *no* and stick out my tongue. The gesture has the desired outcome, and he frowns.

I've had enough of the cute talk with Bash. I almost preferred him when was trying to kill me. I will have my voice back. He can't keep me locked up forever in his rooms.

He shifts and his body goes rigid, unimpressed with my response. He has anger within him he can't control. The origins of his darkness—I recognize it. It's the same darkness that lives within me. He grabs me like I'm a mere feather and throws me three feet to a crumpled heap on the floor. He turns from me, casting his gaze outside. For a moment, he is lost within himself as if feeling remorse from his outburst.

He meets my gaze as I rise and face him. I shift my focus to the sparkling crystal glass holding juice near the tray of food, then back at him. My power is now pulsing through me like razor blades. I could smash that glass and send the shards right into him. Bleed him out as he did Brielle.

He lets out a dark laugh as he stands before me and grips his iron rod in his hand. "Show me, Ophelia." He taunts. "You know you want to. Show me what you can really do. The power you stole from me. I wish to see it."

Goosebumps form on my arms.

He knows—he knew this whole time.

Anger bursts inside me as I focus on the two glasses next to the juice. It was as if we were a couple breaking the fast together. Instead of calling it what it really is—

Captivity.

With my mind, I hurl the glass, causing it to shatter into tiny pieces on the opposite wall. His head turns toward the sound before he shoots his eyes back to mine and smiles.

He cocks a well-manicured brow. "Ophelia?" He drawls, taking a step toward me. "What was that?" He keeps his gaze on me as I twitch my head and raise the second glass. A shatter and a crack as the glass explodes all over the floor.

He watches me with a pleased look, ignoring the thousands of glass shards as I lift them off the ground, creating a swirl and sparkle in the air. I'm only moments from unleashing my fury, sending every single piece into his flesh.

He merely stands unfazed and watches me as these items swirl around him with nothing more than a twitch of my head.

To my surprise, he doesn't cower down. He steps toward me,

places his hand on mine, and traces his fingers up my arms. His face is full of amusement instead of fear.

He keeps his dark gaze locked. "Always full of surprises, aren't we, Ophelia?" he whispers with amazement.

I bite my lips. I wish to kill him. I should kill him. But I freeze into place as he leans down and grabs my hair in his hands. And instead of snapping his neck with my mind as I should, he slides his perfect tongue over my collarbone as he makes his way up to my lips.

A long, deep kiss. I nibble and slide my tongue inside his mouth as the glass in the air drops to the floor in one loud clunk.

I slide my hand down his pants and find his cock is once again hard and lengthened. His eyes grow wild—and it's not my magic that has him desperate for me. It's just me without my voice. What will he do now that he knows the powers in my possession? Will he steal it from me? I just trusted him with my secret.

He kisses my neck and reaches his hands down my side and up my shirt and fondles me. My pussy is pulsing with desire for him. He says he won't fuck me, but how could he not? The need is pouring out of him. I will bring him to his knees before I am done with him.

He will bow before a siren.

"Ophelia," he whispers, as he nuzzles my lips. "That was incredible. I want to see what other powers you possess. What did Ayden give you?"

I part my lips and shake my head, gazing up at him with wide eyes. I feel Ayden's power within me, but it's not within my control. Anger doesn't fuel this power the same way as Bash's.

Bash rubs his finger along my cheekbone. "Take your time, my sweet," he whispers. "We have all day to figure it out."

My heart is pounding a million miles a minute. Only a moment ago, I wanted him dead, and now I want him inside me. This man takes me to both physical and mental extremes.

I wrap my arms around him and slide my tongue into his mouth. It's the first time I've kissed him without his explicit permission, but he lets me. I nibble on his bottom lip and tease my tongue inside his mouth, reminding him of all the ways my tongue makes him squirm. I flicked it on the edge of his cock last night like the true fishy I am.

Right now, I want his lips all over me, to lick me the same way he did last night and give me the same amount of pleasure I've given him. I push his head down and let go, getting lost in the feeling of him. I run my fingers along the hard edges of his body and pull on his dark hair. He trails kisses down my chest while his fingers play at the hemline of my shirt where my pussy is ready and waiting for him. When he gets to my nipples, he moans, biting at their hard edges.

"Ophelia." His voice rumbles with desire, sending shivers down my spine. "Your taste, your scent, everything about you is intoxicating. My powerful little siren, show me what else you can do."

I control the movement of the air outside with my mind. I start softly, creating small gusts of wind, just as I did this morning. Gradually, I intensify my control, pulling the air around until clouds form in the sky. The clouds grow darker and darker as I draw water up from the sea below. My inner power intensifies as I focus my strength on manifesting a thunderstorm over the castle. The storm swirls and darkens the sky above us. Sheets of lightning flash in the air outside. The buildup is gradual at first, but then I release the floodgates and allow the ocean to pour down upon the castle, drenching every single coral stone.

As I work, Bash kisses my body, my neck, and chest. He gets lost in my breasts as I show him how powerful I am. I feel his passion and desire for me, and it fuels me. I want his mouth between my legs while the pressure builds up, causing shockwaves throughout my body. In a split second, I am levitating, weightless, and floating in the air without comprehending how it happened. Bash pulls up my shirt, leaving me exposed in front of him. He kisses my belly with his soft lips as I propel upwards a few inches. He's so lost in me; he doesn't even realize what's happening. Before I know it, my pussy is in line with his face. His lips graze my folds, but it's just enough to send me reeling.

Levitation—Ayden gave me the power to float.

He pauses and looks up at me and flashes a smile as he realizes what I am doing. His tongue flicks my clit before he sticks it inside me and eats me like I'm his morning breakfast.

I silently moan as he squeezes my hips and I wrap my legs around him, and he continues to lick me until I burst. He pulls his tongue out as I hover in the air before him. My chest rises and falls with breaths. He lifts his head up and stares at my body and the power radiating out of me as I wrap myself around him mid-air.

He takes a deep breath and reaches down for his cock. "Screw the law," he says, and his nostrils flare. "I'm going to fuck the shit out of you now, Ophelia."

He pulls away and tries to press my body down a couple of inches. I won't budge. My power is too strong for him to move me. Although I smirk at his feeble attempts. Eventually, he takes his hands and rubs them along my legs. "Can you do me a favor, my sweet, and float that delicious cunt down a few inches for me?"

I channel all the giddy feels I have in this moment and move my body the way he asks so I'm hovering in the air nestling my pussy right at his hard ridge.

The feelings of passion overwhelm me.

Love—love fuels this particular power.

And it consumes me.

He grips my waist and thrusts his cock inside me, and I'm overcome with need as I hover while he fills me. It takes all my strength to keep myself in place, but it's worth it. With each aggressive thrust, I fall deeper and deeper in love with him until I am overwhelmed by the feelings swirling through me.

My feelings for Bash.

He fucks me like this for a few minutes. Full of aggression, passion, and lust. I feel all his emotions within the depths of my core. He wraps his arms around me, and I arch my back to look up at him. He runs his tongue over his teeth and with a glint in his eye he pulls out his cock, and slides his fingers inside me, teasing my clit and gathering my juices on his fingers. I float closer to him, and he cups my cheek. "Open your lips, Ophelia. I want you to taste the power we've given you."

He shoves his fingers into my mouth, and I lick them gleefully. I close my eyes and give him full access to do anything he wants to my body.

I let him defile me.

He fucks and squeezes me until my world darkens, and pussy explodes. Orgasm after orgasm rolls through me in the most intense way, as my magic strengthens. If I were a mere human, I'd be dead. His iron grip and anger combined with this thread of magic would break a girl to pieces.

But I am strong—I'm a siren. He fucks me till I can't take it any longer and fall in a jumbled heap at his feet. With a twist in my stomach, I glance up at him as he holds the rod in his hands with a dark smile on his face and beads of sweat pour down his neck.

All my power completely sucked out of me.

It's then I realize despite how strong I am, I am completely and hopelessly in love with Bash Throdos and am once again under his control.

Chapter Fourteen

OPHELIA

B ash stares down at me, and a smile plays at his lips. He stole
them—my powers, as I knew he would. Deep inside, I had
a glimmer of hope that he wouldn't take them. The moment I
realized what triggered my levitation, he owned me. He didn't have
to seize them, as I now have an insatiable desire to please him.

Calm, careful, and controlled, he bends down and picks me up
as I lie panting on the floor. I stare back at him, vulnerable and
exposed. My body still pulsing from what it just endured.

Devine. Sex with Bash is heavenly. My power making it even
more so.

He says nothing as he brings me back to his bed and places me
down, then undresses and crawls in next to me. He absently stares
out at the ocean, his eyes darkening as he watches the puffy clouds
of my storm dissipate. I nestle in beside him and rest my head
against the crook of his arm.

He will surely kill me now. I had my chance, and I squandered it, all because of his pretty dark eyes and orgasmic tongue or how his voice can send me to another world. Now he knows all my secrets and what I am capable of. I showed him my abilities; he knows the full extent of what I can do.

He balls his fingers in one hand and wraps his arm around me with the other, drawing circles on my arm and waist. He's twitching—a nervous tick and says nothing to me.

After a few minutes, he whispers, "What to do with you, Ophelia?"

That silky voice.

I lean up and kiss the bare skin of his neck. I do so to remind him I am his, and I must show him all the ways I can make him happy.

He feels it—he must. Our lovemaking was not some menial fuck. I've had sex with plenty of sailors to know the difference. It means something. He cannot just toss me away. Which is why he hasn't looked at me in ten minutes as my fingers circle his chest. I play with his hair and lie with my leg entwined around him.

He may hold all my powers close to his chest, but the power of a woman's allure can never be stolen. I know how much Bash desires me—even if he doesn't want to admit it; he shows me with his cock, teeth, and tongue.

Our eyes finally meet, and to my surprise, he shifts and leans over, grabbing his magical rod with my powers trapped inside. My heart tightens and skips a beat. I've longed for my powers more than the air that fills my lungs. The constant pain in my heart is a dark void from the depths of hell. I miss my voice most of all.

He places his hand on my back. "I'm going to give you your voice back now, Ophelia. But only for a few moments. If you try to use it against me, I will take it back again and give it to the Coral Throne, where it actually belongs. Do you understand?"

I nod eagerly.

He flicks his wrist and releases silver mist into my lungs. I breathe deeply, the tingle of its power sweet and sultry as it passes through my blood. If only he would return my other two powers to me, as they are rightfully mine.

I flit my gaze to him and arch one brow. His name rolls off my tongue. "Bash." I've not called him Bash since he asked me to the night I got here.

He merely smirks and plays with a lock of my hair before cupping my face. "Oh, how I missed your voice, my sweet. I have so many questions."

I sit up and fold my arms. "Me first."

This is the first true conversation we've had. Before he stole my voice, he was dominating me, and we really only had our first night together in the tavern and our night of dancing before his true dark nature shined through. I wasn't allowed to speak and when I did, I couldn't call him by his name.

A smirk spreads across his handsome, dark face. So eager to listen.

My head cocks to the side. "Why do you make me call you *my king*, when you are not the king?"

An honest, curious question.

He slides closer and grabs my hands, playing with my fingers, and doesn't respond.

"Answer my question, Bash."

He sighs. "Because that is what I am, my sweet. I am the true king of Atlantis."

I purse my lips in deep thought as I behold him with his head hanging low. Bash lies, just as Lady Alana lied before him. The crown prince has always been Alexander, as was his father before him. Bash has no direct claim to the throne that I know of.

"But what about Alexander?" I dare to ask.

Even speaking his name brings bile to my throat.

The Coral Throne doesn't lie—everyone knows that. It ordains and is the reason the Throdos family is so powerful; it chose them. If King Alex wasn't meant to be king, he wouldn't be.

It's as simple as that.

A flash of darkness hits his eyes, and his face tightens. "It was the night before my father's coronation. The day after my grandfather passed," he tells me gently.

I remember hearing about that day. King Sebastian III was an admirable king. He stood on his morals, and the gods favored him.

He continues tracing his fingers up my thigh. "My father was usurped before he even had a chance. My uncle was waiting in the shadows. He had a whole army of people to support him. The court prevented a drunken ruler by killing him the day before his coronation. They claimed he had a terrible accident because of excessive amounts of wine and fell off his balcony. But they murdered him. I watched them do it. I was in the secret passageways my father showed me. The same ones I used to bring you here. Though no one would ever believe me. I was not yet of age, so my uncle assumed responsibilities and gave the legacy to his son instead. He changed the bloodline. My mother was a mess. She died a few months later from a broken heart."

My heart aches for him—for the suffering Bash must have endured as a boy.

"Why didn't you take the crown when you came of age? Why

aren't you king now, Bash? If this is as you say?"

He reaches for me and gathers me in his arms.

"I didn't want it at the time. I decided that day I never wanted the burden of being king. I wanted Alex to have it, so I never contested him for it. In fact, I bent my knee on my eighteenth birthday nearly ten years ago and declared my loyalty to him as the crowned prince in front of the entire kingdom. If I try to get it back now, it would be considered treason. The people would never allow it. If Alex dies, the crown goes to Ayden."

I don't believe him. He wouldn't play these bedroom games with me if he didn't desire even a sliver of power.

"What of the Coral Throne?" I ask. "Shouldn't it's ancient power decide who is the true king?"

He tenderly pulls my hair from my eyes. "Smart little fishy trying to get information from me, aren't you?"

I don't deny it.

"And what of you, my Ophelia? What are you exactly? I've seen a few sirens trapped in our castle over the years, but none who have your particular abilities." He dangles the silver rod. "Naughty girl stealing our dormant powers like that."

Dormant powers.

He presses his lips to my brow. "You came for that raven-haired oceanid we found in the bay years ago. You came to avenge her."

Not a question.

I nod and hitch a breath. "Yes, she is . . . was my sister."

He squeezes me as I rest my head on his chest and listen to his thundering heartbeat. "And how did you know who I was?" he asks, his breath tickling my cheek. "What made you choose me the other night at the tavern?"

I draw my hands to his leg and tease my fingers up to his cock. "I suspected when I saw you. I heard the Royal Adviser was handsome and liked to frequent the tavern to find whores. I opted to take my chance."

He snickers. "Smart girl."

Anger pulses inside me, and I squeeze his cock a little harder than I should. "I could have killed you when you kissed me in the hallway of the tavern. You were under my spell even then, Bash. I could have slit your throat and been rid of you."

He runs his hand up to my breast and squeezes. "But aren't you glad you didn't?"

I turn from him, facing away. No more games—no more fun. I'll not play along any longer, not until he tells me what happened to Brielle.

He presses himself up behind me, his warmth wraps around me. A few minutes of silence brings tears to my eyes and intensifies my anger.

My weak *human* emotions—

I did nothing to avenge Brielle. Instead, I fell for a king without a throne. Tiny sobs squeak out of me. I wish he would take back my voice then kill me. Anything is better than this.

He grabs my shoulder and runs his hand down my spine, and I remain stiff as a board even as his soft hands bring a tingle to my skin.

"Ophelia," he whispers, nuzzling his mouth on my ear. "I was not the one to kill her."

I face him, my eyes glisten and plead as he gazes back at me. Right now, I'm not an oceanid. I'm not a siren who can steal powers. I'm a girl whose life is in the hands of the man I love. He gets to choose whether I live or die.

I whisper and my voice only breaks. "I have no one, Bash. Just kill me, please. Don't give me to him."

He rolls me onto my back and slides on top of me with a dark gleam in his eye. "He knows you're here, Ophelia. I had to tell him about what you did to Fredrick. There is no going back now. He'll check on you once his evening affairs are settled."

I pound my tiny fists into his chest. Desperate, angry, pathetic, and doing very little to actually hurt him. He takes it—he lets me hit him with all my pathetic human strength.

"Why, Bash?" I scream and thrash. "You already control me. Let me stay here with you. Tell them I fled, that I left the castle. No one needs to know. I'm yours, Bash. I'm only yours."

He grabs my fists and squeezes them, moving them down to his side. "Because of my loyalty to him," he says darkly. "My loyalty to Atlantis and to the Coral Throne, even if it kills me inside for what he will do to you. You are the enemy, Ophelia. I can't change fate or a thousand years of history. Sirens will be our undoing—that is the prophecy." He cocks a brow. "I don't wish to see that happen in my lifetime, so I must end you."

My chest tightens and for the first time with Bash, fear courses through my veins. I thrash and I kick at him as my voice bundles up in my throat, awaiting its release.

"I'll sing, Bash." It's an empty, desperate threat. "I'll sing, and then I'll kill you. I won't go back in there."

He snickers. "There's my feisty girl." He pins me down. "You won't, Ophelia. Because you have no control here." His pupils flare, and he pulls my hands over my head. "And remember how mad I get when you say no to me?"

I press my lips together as he squeezes my neck, and my vision goes dark. My pussy throbs as he brings me to my brink. My lips quiver as he pulls himself away, and my head hangs loose.

Broken.

I find his gaze and see pain clearly etched on his face. I try to call out to him, one last plea. Then instead of bringing me back again as he usually does, everything goes black.

Chapter Fifteen

OPHELIA

My eyes flutter open as cold air wraps around me. My face is pressed up on the slippery hard stone of my water prison. I'm completely naked once more and in my human form. I can barely breathe as I bring my fingers to the little muscles at the front of my throat where Bash squeezed the life out of me. Somewhere nearby water trickles, and that's the sound that brings me back from the brink.

Drop. Drop. Drop.

My siren sings from within.

He did it—he handed me over to Alexander and put me back in this pit. After everything we went through the past two days. Does he feel nothing? Is he that desperate for dominance? Surely, he can find some other fucked up whore who frequents the taverns. I know three who would enjoy Bash's type of pleasure. Why would he do this? I would have given him everything he wanted.

I would have given him my soul.

I stare out of the circular drain that leads into the ocean below. I barely blink or move, and I certainly can't breathe. They won't even give me water to let me die in my true form. Bash deprived me of my voice as well. At least he left me a tiny light—a flicker of a single candle. I hold on to that light.

I'm sorry, Papa. I'm sorry, Brielle. I failed us.

Bash doesn't deserve me. His inability to stand up to the false king shows his weakness. He should hold all the power. Instead, he seems to cower to it. I simply refuse to believe he feels nothing for me. The way he held me, looked at me—made love to me. I felt it as true as the power of my siren's voice. Bash is the first person I'll come for if I survive. I have a special plan for how I will break him down limb by limb, starting with his cock.

My ears twitch as the sound of water echoes around me. I scramble to my feet as the water fills the pool around me and I spot a lone figure watching me from outside the glass wall.

Bash.

He stands with his head tilted to one side, his dark hair covering his eyes, and his face expressionless. As the water engulfs me, I transform in front of him, giving my body a powerful surge of energy as my tail glistens and glows its purple hues. I keep my eyes on him as my body elongates.

I bare my teeth and whip my tail into the glass. Bash can't help but flinch at my fury. Ancient magic is the only thing keeping him alive—normally my tail would have broken this glass and severed off his head.

A shadow hovers behind him—Bash is not alone. A man, taller, with longer golden hair and a crown that lays upon his wicked head. King Alexander stares at me in wonder—his eyes full of both malice and hunger.

I spin around and circle the small space. The energy I have in this form makes it hard to stay in one place. I circle at least twenty times as the two mightiest men in Atlantis behold me.

Bash simply turns away from me and leaves into the darkness. Leaves me alone with the wicked false king who killed Brielle and is about to kill me.

The king draws his eyes at me—inspects me. I have no idea what to expect from him; I suspect my womanly allure won't work on him quite the same way as Bash or Ayden. I pace back and forth in my pit; I circle my prey as he watches me.

Eventually, he pulls the lever, draining the water. Bash forced me to prove what I am, leaving me with nothing. No voice, powers, or fin. I should be scared—frightened beyond belief. But I'm not. I've resolved to my fate and refuse to show him fear. Bash hasn't taken everything from me. I still have one tiny speck of hope.

Once the water is gone, Alexander steps through a glass door. I close my eyes as his rough hands grab me, and he shoves me up a set of stairs to a stone room with a single bench with torches lit on either side. I don't try to stop him. This needs to end no matter the outcome.

The stench of moldy water collapses my lungs as it drips around us. No wonder Bash didn't want to keep me here.

Vile, wretched—*smell of death*.

I would have preferred if Bash kept me here instead of bringing me to his rooms and treating me like a queen. A better reminder of the true depths of his monstrous nature.

I keep my eyes closed as Alexander cups my face—his hands are softer than I thought him capable of. When I open my eyes and meet his gaze, Brielle's pain overwhelms me. He has a curious look on his face.

He draws in a long breath. "You killed my seer."

I bare my teeth at him, and he pulls his hand away as if surprised I would have a reaction to him. He snorts and grabs my lips and squeezes with all his brute strength. "You will answer me, you siren bitch. I am your king."

He lets go of me, and I spit at him. *Stupid man*—he doesn't even realize Bash stole my voice or the control Bash has over me with that cylinder. He is clueless as to how much power Bash has. Plus, I will never bow to this king—not when I serve another. Even with all my hatred, I know deep in my heart I will always serve Bash.

Alex shoves me headfirst into the wall. Searing pain tears through me as my skull cracks and bleeds out from the stone. I let the blood trickle down my cheek before I taste it.

My powerful blood—

I lie on the cold, hard ground as Alexander hovers above me. His crown and cape glimmer in the flickering light. His long, golden hair flowing from some unknown draft of air. If it was Bash who just hurt me, he'd be kind after. His loving hands would heal me—soothe me.

Not Alexander.

He merely snickers as the light dances on the hard edges of his face. He wipes the blood from my cheek with his thumb and presses it into his mouth, licking my blood off his fingers. He savors it.

"Stupid siren cunt," he says, "sneaking inside my castle. I will kill you for what you did to my seer and for bewitching my brothers. You seductive little whore."

I turn to face him as I lie on the floor and prop my hands up as my long, raven hair falls just over the curves of my supple breasts. And he notices—he can't take his eyes off them. Batting my eyes won't work on him, but I can remind him when I'm in my human form, I am most definitely womanly.

Just for a moment, I need him to forget what I am and focus on the tight pussy he won't refuse. He won't fuck a siren—but he will fuck a girl. A split second is all I need to destroy them all.

Alexander lifts me up and places me on the stone bench and then grabs me by the chin once more.

He grins. "Do you have any idea what I do to creatures like you?"

I try to turn my head, but his grip is too tight. He keeps me locked in his brutal gaze.

"I kill you—I drain every drop of your blood and store it away."

Evil—sinister man.

I bite his flesh—I rip my teeth right into his arm, tearing at his skin. He cries out, curls his lip, and strikes me—my head whips to the side, but I revel in the pain and hold my head up high. My mother was a siren *queen*. I'm stronger than he realizes.

I shift and bend my knees, opening myself up to him. The bulge in his pants lets me know my actions have the desired effect. He glares at me, and I part my lips, licking the little drops of blood still dripping in my mouth as I pet myself between my legs. He bends to his knees before me, trailing his hands up my thighs to get a better look.

Come on now, wicked heir—you know you want me.

He snarls his lip. "Bash and Ayden told me, but I couldn't quite believe it. A siren with a human pussy."

I spread my legs slightly but then remember men like him, like damsels in distress. So, I pretend to fight it and clench my legs together.

He tightens his jaw. "You stupid whore—you spread your legs for them. You will do so for me."

He pulls down his pants and pulls out his pathetic, throbbing cock. No wonder he has a complex in the bedroom. That thing couldn't do damage if it tried.

He shoves his fingers deep inside me. I close my eyes, pretending it's Bash as he twists and plays with me. Unlike Bash, where my body would melt at his touch—with Alexander, all I feel is rippling pain. Brielle's pain and the sirens he killed before her. I hold on to that feeling because it reminds me I'm still alive.

I keep my eyes closed as his body presses in on me and he lays me down on the cold stone floor. The King of Atlantis—fucking his prisoner on a wretched, dirty prison floor. Bash at least showed some class by taking me to a better room.

My chest tightens as he readies himself.

I know I have him. He can't control his primal desires. Right now, I'm simply a woman for his taking. He shoves himself deep inside and grunts and thrusts as my body betrays me, and my pussy tightens around him.

I feel nothing—just a dark void as he fucks me. Neither as warm as Ayden nor as explosive as Bash. Just his limp, sad length barely filling my insides.

I sense it like before with the others. This power does not trickle in. Instead, it sends shock waves through me, and I know exactly what feeling I must pull on to fuel it.

Despair.

Despite my overwhelming sadness, I smile as his vile body quivers, and he grunts while he cums all over me.

He's the last piece of my puzzle—my final power.

When he's done, he lifts off me with a sneer on his face. I feel the buzz of energy ignite within me, the power searing inside me. Ready to unleash.

I open my mouth and smile, and he narrows his eyes as he tucks himself back in.

His eyes burn with rage. "What are you smiling at, you siren slut?"

I lick my lips and unleash it on him. His own power—used against him. I unleash all my anger, rage, love, hurt, sadness, every emotion bundled up deep within me and explode it out of my body. The electric current flows out of my hands right into him. The room explodes around me as I push all its force to kill this detestable king.

The light is blinding, but when the room dims, I regain my senses.

I choke on air when I see him staring back at me, smiling—unaffected by the storm of energy I just inflicted on him.

My anger and despair turn to fear as the dark king chuckles and leans forward, pressing his lips into my ear. "Your powers don't affect me. It didn't for any of the sea sluts before you either."

It doesn't work—my powers can't kill the king.

His eyes flash as he pulls out a silver dagger. The same one I stole from the seer. I let out a silent scream as he digs it into my side, slicing open my belly. My body pulses as my blood floods out of me. He then stabs and twists the knife on my other side. He stands back as blood pools beneath me, and Atticus comes from the shadows to scoop it up and puts it in a bucket.

Before my world goes black, my consciousness slips to some-where inherently different. A place that transcends darkness.

I only hold on by thinking of Brielle—and in the deepest part of my mind, it's Bash's face that consumes my mind.

Chapter Sixteen

BASH

The Coral Throne is cold as I lounge upon it, resting my legs over the side. I sit here sometimes, usually late at night, dreaming of being the king. That feeling used to sicken me, the thought of responsibility. Now it's all I think about.

I stare out to the empty throne room beyond; the moonlight shining down from the open pillars above on the mosaic floors knowing down below where Alex is likely killing her or fucking her. Ophelia's silent screams rip through my heart.

It sickens me—all of it. Even though I understand the reasons behind it, especially with the looming threat of war that hovers around us. Siren blood equals healing powers. Alexander can now bring his army back from the dead.

There are so many more humane ways to do it. Alex is so twisted about it. Insisting on killing them despite others being able to do it just as easily, Atticus would have no qualms about it. The throne has darkened his soul beyond repair.

I wait for Alex to finish with her. Just like I did with the last one—Brielle, her name was, so I've learned. Pain twists and turns in my gut, thinking of my sweet Ophelia in his arms, and it pains me beyond belief. My feelings for her have taken me off guard, and I never would have let him have her if it didn't serve my agenda and oath to my father to protect this city at all costs.

Except Ophelia isn't the enemy—she is the weapon. And one I've fallen deeply in love with. I needed to finish building her so I can fight the true enemy of this city.

The false king Alexander.

So, I turned her over to him with the assumption he will break his own rule and fuck her as I know he fucks all of them. I've never known how he fucks them in their fishy form, but I suspect he's done it all along. When this is all done, I hope Ophelia will find it in her heart to forgive me.

Alexander's voice cuts through me. "You're in my spot, Bash."

I drift my gaze to meet him and arch a singular brow at the way his crown lays crooked upon his head. "Am I now?" I rise and bow to him. "Apologies, your *highness*."

He grumbles and takes his place on the throne. "Enough, Bash. I know you liked this one. But it is done. She is dead as she should be."

I flick my wrist. "She's a fish, Alex. I will never and could never like a fish."

He curls his lip, but a dark gleam hints at his eyes. "I'll forgive you this one time for not telling me about her sooner. I understand she was different."

He has no idea.

"She had us all fooled," I retort.

His eyes flash, and he shifts his gaze beyond the throne, to the open air, the sea, and city below us. "How many do you think there are? Those that walk among us? These . . . half-breed mutants?"

I suppress my rage at his mention of her in this way. She is perfection. How does he not see the value she could bring us? This army from the south would stand no chance if she were to unleash her fury upon it.

I shrug. "I don't know. It's hard enough to catch a siren and have them not kill you. I can't imagine how one would fornicate with one. Let alone have two children."

Oops, that was a slip.

He narrows his eyes. "Two of them, you say?"

I roll my eyes. A false king and a daft one indeed. "The hair color, Alex. The way she snuck into the castle, knowing how much danger she was in. She was clearly related to the last one."

He scoffs and lounges on the throne. "I suppose."

I take a few steps away. "Are you finished with her, then?"

A sparkling smile forms on his lips, which sickens me. "Once they're done with the blood, send your twins to dispose of the body." He gives an evil grin. "I got a lot of her blood. Our stores are replenished."

I cringe at the thought of my beautiful Ophelia's blood stored and blended in with all the rest. My jaw flexes and I nod. "As you wish."

"Oh, and Bash?"

I slap a fake smile on my face. "What is it, Alex?"

"If you ever lie to me again, I will behead you. I can't let it get out that my Royal Adviser commits treason without punishment. Next time you find one, you find me immediately."

A twist in my gut, not from fear, but rage. How *dare* this false king threaten me?

I simply bow. "It won't happen again."

I disappear through the silent castle and slip into my rooms. Alex will have someone watch me—that I am sure of. I saw the flash of distrust in his eyes. He'll never trust me the same way again.

Once I'm secure in my rooms, I wait before slipping into my hidden corridors. Another secret, along with my magic cylinder, meant only for the true king.

When I reach the prison, my body tenses at the sight of her. He left her to rot. Her beautiful body—like silk just lying on the stone floor of the dungeon. Even in death, her lips shine bright, and her lashes lay on her eyes, dark and thick. Her raven hair, like midnight rain, casts down over her naked body. Every drop of her blood was stolen from her, but I only need one to revive her—just one. Hopefully, Alex didn't suck her completely dry. He has no idea how precious she is—how valuable and powerful she is. He doesn't deserve her; not like I do.

I lean down and gather her in my arms. She's cold to the touch—her body is like enchanted ice. The cylinder in my pocket vibrates—it pulls and tugs. It purrs.

She has a power within her. In her last breaths, she stole it from Alexander as I hoped she would. I feel it within her. I hope she can understand why I did this. Why it had to be this way. I pull out the cylinder and release the magic held within.

Her magic—her voice, the telekinesis she stole from me, and the levitation from Ayden. And whatever power she stole from Alex. I give it all back to her.

Her body shakes as the energy courses through her—the one

drop of blood left in her is enough to revive her. I feel for her pulse—it's weak, but it's there.

I let out a sigh of relief. Alex is as sloppy a murderer as he is a king. He left some blood in her.

"Come now, my sweet," I whisper to her. Her body heats, and I know she is still here with me. The magic of the Coral Throne reviving her from true death. She will come back to me.

I take her through the hidden tunnels and corridors back upstairs to my room. Once I'm there, I place her on my bed and tuck her hair behind her ear.

Even in death, her beauty shines—her body glows like the coral sea.

I have no idea how long it will take until she's back with me, but I will nurse her and hide her as long as she needs. I pull one of my tunics out of the wardrobe and dress her. Then I rest beside her, admiring the curves of her beautiful body.

Alexander made a grave mistake by not dripping her dry. She'll be my greatest weapon once I rebuild her. Perhaps even stronger than the Coral Throne itself. And one I will have complete control over.

I'll reclaim what's rightfully mine and bring this city back to glory. I will rule as I always was meant to. I'll have her by my side through it all.

Ophelia will not only be my weapon—she will be my queen.

Chapter Seventeen

BASH

Three nights have passed since I saved Ophelia. Three days of listening to Alex's painful whining at court about his betrothed, and my complete facade as I dutifully advise the false king on trivial matters of a phantom threat from the south, while the real threat is within his own castle walls. I had to fuck Lady Lillian to appease my cousins. To show the court how nothing has changed, and Bash is still Bash. I had to hold Lillian on my lap at dinner while my heart and head were with someone else.

Everything has changed. I have something to live for. A purpose.

I go to Ophelia every night and don't allow anyone in my room. The lack of change in her concerns me. Only her small pulse indicates life within her. So, I hold on to that thread of hope she will not die. I lie beside her, and I don't touch her. Only happy to be near her.

On the third night, I walk into my room, and my pulse thickens. *Ophelia is gone.*

I jerk my head around the room. The sunken bath on my balcony is empty. No sign of her anywhere. But she can't leave without my consent—the wards in my room won't allow it.

I click my tongue. "Ophelia. I know you're here. Can we talk about it?"

When I lift my gaze, she is there, and I am stunned at the sight of her.

She hovers in the corner near the ceiling, nine feet above the ground. She still wears my shirt, which barely covers her, and her strong bare legs lengthen beneath her.

And she glows—an electric current hovers around her.

Almost feline, she falls onto the bed and jumps to all fours, whipping her head up. She glares at me, and my cock instantly comes to life. The energy in her eyes—if looks could kill, my soul would burn in hell. Even so, I'm in for it. I will not leave this room unscathed, I'm sure.

Her voice is soft but poisonous. "Why did you bring me back from the dead, Bash?" She cocks her head, waiting for my response, and a fire flickers in that immortal gaze.

My beautiful queen of the sea is reborn.

I merely smile. "Don't be so dramatic, my sweet. You weren't dead, per se. You wouldn't be speaking to me right now if you were."

Like a bolt of lightning, she is on me. She flies to me and wraps her legs tightly around me. I know she will try to kill me, but my cock pulses anyway. I wrap my arms around her and squeeze her bare bottom and smile as I feel her soft skin beneath my fingernails as I dig them into her flesh. She still smells of junipers from the oils of my tub.

She leans up and whispers in my ear. "The hardest decision is how to kill you, Bash."

The throbbing in my groin becomes unbearable at how utterly sexy those words are.

She falls off me, landing on her feet, and I keep my arms wrapped around her. She rubs her hands along my waistband, keeping her emerald gaze locked in on me.

She parts her lips. "I could snap your neck with my eyes." She runs her arm down my torso. "I could pull your body apart limb by limb and suck the oxygen out of your blood." She teases her fingers down my groin. "Or I could throw you into the sea and drown you."

I nearly come undone. I have to press my teeth into my bottom lip to not explode. Not being the dominant one makes me breathless with excitement. The thrill of what she might do to me, the malice in her words.

I stand perfectly still as her soft hands finally graze down and she unbuttons my pants, pulling out my now rock-hard length. She grabs me and presses her lips into mine, teasing me with her tongue. I match her motions, sucking on her gorgeous lips.

She flashes her pearly white teeth. "Or I could just do this."

She zaps me—a bolt of light flows through her fingers and she burns my cock. The pain is excruciating. A fiery sensation shoots up my spine and explodes in my head. Her glowing face is all I see as my knees lock, and the room comes into focus.

Electricity.

Alex gave her the power of Zeus himself, the ultimate power of the king. Her beautiful face shows no love for me, but I deserved it. I deserve any punishment she wishes to bestow on me. I'd even face death if that is what would please her.

I bow before her and press my hands into her thighs as she hovers a couple of inches in the air. I lean my head into her stomach.

I bow before my queen.

She lowers down and lifts my head as she peers at me. Glimpses of my old Ophelia stare back at me. Hurt betrays her eyes. "Why did you do it?" she asks me in a pained voice that breaks my heart. "I trusted you, Bash. I gave myself to you and you were supposed to protect me."

My hands run up her legs until they rest upon her hips. I will spend the rest of my days protecting her if she will let me.

I close my eyes. "I gave you freedom, Ophelia, and your final power. Alex thinks you're dead. If I didn't give him to you, you never would have left this castle—the ancient power wouldn't allow it. It still won't allow it, I'm afraid, but now you can remain invisible within these walls. I have the means to hide you." My eyes open, and I peer up at her. "Look at you now, Ophelia. More power than you know what to do with. You are reborn, my love. This was your destiny."

She follows my gaze to the window just as the final streaks of light disappear into the midnight sky. I rise and pull her into me. She softens and nuzzles her body next to mine. "I have so many plans for you, Ophelia," I whisper.

Her lips curl. "So, I am still a prisoner, then?" she asks icily.

I run my hands down her arm. "That is out of my control, I'm afraid. The power you hold binds you here. You will become a creature of the castle—like Atticus, like the seer you killed. The Coral Throne has claimed you, Ophelia. You must serve it."

Her eyes gleam. "I must serve Alex then, since it's he who sits on the throne."

Those words nearly kill me, and I resist the sudden urge to shove my hands down her throat. To remind her of her place in the bedroom and her place with me. She had her moment of fun. I bowed to her once—it's just not my cup of tea.

I grab her and throw her on my bed, pressing my arm down on her slender body. I don't hold back the force within me. She hisses and bites at me, but still . . . she takes it. Even with all her powers, she likes my domination. I need to remind her what I can do to her with my tongue, and the fact I can snatch her powers with a single flick of my wrist should she ever use them on me. Although I never plan to stifle her powers again. I like her better in her true form.

I arch my brow and gaze down at her. "So, what do you say, Ophelia? Will you help me get my throne back?"

She blinks, her body pulsating with the power she could use to destroy anyone in her wake. It's then I feel her weaken beneath me. Her body trembles and her limbs go limp.

"What is it?" I ask her, easing my pressure slightly. "What is wrong, my sweet?"

She tenses beneath me. "I have to leave, Bash. This power is overwhelming. I need to go to the sea and feel my tail and fins. In this form, I don't feel like myself. Human emotions are too intense. This world isn't mine anymore." She rises and walks to the balcony—still wearing my shirt and only my shirt. "I'll be back, Bash. One day soon."

I lift my gaze. "What are you going to do, Ophelia? You can't leave the barrier."

She blinks and her mighty power shines within her eyes. "I'm going to find my mother, then I'll come back and rip Alex's throat apart for what he did to me."

I shake my head. "It won't be that easy, my sweet. He's powerful, more than you understand. Your magic won't work on him the way it does with me. He is protected while he sits on the throne."

She sweetly smiles. "Well, I guess we will have to dethrone him then, won't we? You are the true king, Bash. Get your throne back."

Like a wisp of the wind, she is gone. I run to the window and see her running down the stone stairs to the city and sea beyond, her black hair swirling behind her. As she disappears from my view, I can imagine her running into the sea, turning into the magnificent creature that she is.

A hole forms in my heart as I ponder her words.

Dethrone King Alexander.

Is it possible? Can I really do it?

I'll be the king she needs. I'm more powerful than she realizes. Once I ascend to the throne, I will wield power equal to hers.

And together, we will be unstoppable.

Other Works by Rhea Ryan

The Bone Love Duet

Pretty Little Island (Book 1)

Pretty Little Island (The Bone Love Duet Book 1) (geni.us)
Torn between two lovers on a pretty but deadly island, London
King must survive the ravages of the wilderness and a battle for her
heart.My first day at New Ocean Prep was supposed to be a fresh
start. A chance to return to my hometown—leaving my ruined life
behind me. My goal is simple. Keep my grades up, my head down,
and focus on securing my spot in a top journalism program.My
past catches up with me as I'm drawn towards the two hottest
hockey players in school. A trip to a national hockey tournament
in Alaska has me investigating the truth behind what happened to

a girl they tormented and killed two summers earlier.This story has more layers than I imagined. The deeper I enter their world, the stronger our bonds become until I can't tell whose side I'm really on.

About the Author

Rhea Ryan is a spicy writer of romance on the edge of dark and twisty. Her stories are a masterful exploration of the human heart, skillfully navigating the complex and often grey terrain of our inner lives. After writing in the corporate world for over a decade, she realized she had a desire and compulsion to write creatively. She lives in Western Canada with her husband, two young children and a fur baby.

.

www.ingramcontent.com/pod-product-compliance
Lightning Source LLC
Chambersburg PA
CBHW051958170626
46808CB00007B/2680